W9-BLI-100

"You're marrying me."

Whatever else Zade had said could not have shocked Catrina as much as that. He didn't love her; she wasn't sure he even liked her. He had wanted her, but she was even uncertain about that now.

"We don't love each other," she whispered shakily, immediately on the defensive, and he suddenly smiled down at her grimly, reaching out and pulling her toward him until she was enclosed in hard arms that offered nothing but possession.

"I'm not even certain what love is," he confessed in ironic amusement. "It seems to me to be one of the few things I haven't experienced. I know what I want, though. I want a wife who can burn up in my arms, meet desire with desire. I work hard and live lonely. Now I've got you."

Dear Reader,

Harlequin Romance would like to welcome you back to the ranch again with our yearlong miniseries **Hitched!** We've rounded up twelve of our most popular authors, and the result is a whole year of romance Western style: cool cowboys, rugged ranchers and, of course, the women who tame them.

Next month's title is Rebecca Winters's *The Badlands Bride* (#3409). Xan knew that Judd Coltrain, with his deep sexy drawl and rugged good looks, was the perfect man to be the father of her children. But was Judd the simple rancher he seemed?

Look out for books branded **Hitched!** in the coming months. We'll be featuring books by all your favorite authors: Ruth Jean Dale, Val Daniels and Heather Allison, to mention a few!

Happy reading!

The Editors
Harlequin Romance

How the West was wooed!

A Dangerous Magic
Patricia Wilson

Harlequin Books

TORONTO • NEW YORK • LONDON
AMSTERDAM • PARIS • SYDNEY • HAMBURG
STOCKHOLM • ATHENS • TOKYO • MILAN
MADRID • WARSAW • BUDAPEST • AUCKLAND

If you purchased this book without a cover you should be aware
that this book is stolen property. It was reported as "unsold and
destroyed" to the publisher, and neither the author nor the
publisher has received any payment for this "stripped book."

ISBN 0-373-03405-9

A DANGEROUS MAGIC

First North American Publication 1996.

Copyright © 1993 by Patricia Wilson.

All rights reserved. Except for use in any review, the reproduction or
utilization of this work in whole or in part in any form by any electronic,
mechanical or other means, now known or hereafter invented, including
xerography, photocopying and recording, or in any information storage
or retrieval system, is forbidden without the written permission of the
publisher, Harlequin Enterprises Limited, 225 Duncan Mill Road,
Don Mills, Ontario, Canada M3B 3K9.

All characters in this book have no existence outside the imagination of
the author and have no relation whatsoever to anyone bearing the same
name or names. They are not even distantly inspired by any individual
known or unknown to the author, and all incidents are pure invention.

This edition published by arrangement with Harlequin Books S.A.

® and TM are trademarks of the publisher. Trademarks indicated with
® are registered in the United States Patent and Trademark Office, the
Canadian Trade Marks Office and in other countries.

Printed in U.S.A.

CHAPTER ONE

GARY came in from the yard in a flurry of wind and biting cold; even from the kitchen they could feel the sharp, bitter blast.

'A touch of snow in the air,' he said worriedly, walking over to drop a kiss on Catrina's upturned face. 'Hope we're not going to be back to that,' he added, glancing at his mother, who was busy at the cooker. 'It's cold enough as it is for the lambs.'

'Well, March is a sneaky month even late on, especially up in these dales,' Mrs Hudson pointed out, handing him a hot mug of tea. 'You'd better be getting off home, Catrina, before you're stuck here all night.'

They both heard the disapproval in her voice and Gary winked at Catrina behind his mother's back.

'She'll be stuck here all night and every night in two months' time,' he said with a grin. 'As far as I'm concerned she could just move in now and be done with it.'

'If you're going to tease,' his mother said tightly, 'I'd be pleased if you'd keep off vulgar subjects.'

'What's vulgar about it?' Gary protested. 'We're engaged and in two months we'll be married. Most people of our age just live together.'

'Not in this dale,' Mrs Hudson snapped, not at all amused at his breezy goading. 'Time enough for that when I've moved out. You'll have the house to yourselves, never fear.'

Catrina felt uncomfortable. It was not an unusual situation. She hated it when they started like this, Gary teasing and grinning, his mother primly disapproving.

It was a good thing that Mrs Hudson would be moving out and letting them have the farm to themselves when they married. Not that she was moving far. The cottage she would occupy was next door, actually attached to the main farmhouse.

Gary pointed that out in amusement and his mother went back to the cooker, her lips set firmly.

'You'll need me. I'm farm born and bred, like you. Catrina is a town girl and she says she's not giving her job up anyway.' It was a deliberate attempt to cause friction but Gary never rose to the bait. He was quite proud that Catrina was the town librarian, even if it was only a small library.

'Why should she?' he asked in his usual good-humoured way. 'Finally she will, of course. Then you'll be close enough to be a ready-made baby-sitter.'

It didn't bring a smile of anticipation to his mother's face and Catrina shot Gary a reproving look. This bickering was something she would never get used to. He merely winked at her again and Mrs Hudson went on, 'I don't know why you want a May wedding. It's not always warm in May. August's best, more flowers out and sure weather. Catrina's mother would have chosen August, I bet.'

It wiped the smile from Gary's face and he reached out to take Catrina's hand as she winced. It was only a year since her mother had died and she still felt raw about it, as Gary knew. The remark had been typical of the small digs Gary's mother tried from time to time.

'We do our own arranging,' he said sharply. 'There's no way that we're waiting until August. We've waited long enough.'

Conversation stopped and Gary drank his tea with a tight expression on his face. There was one thing about it: he always came out on Catrina's side. She would never have to battle with his mother by herself. She looked across at him with warm, dark eyes, watching the lamp-light catch the shine of his fair hair. Gary was a lovely person and she was lucky to be marrying him. He looked up and caught her gaze, his expression lightening.

'Hey! News, news, and I forgot to tell you. Zade's coming!'

'All the way from America?' Catrina asked in aston-ishment. She had never ceased to be told about Gary's cousin Zade, his childhood hero. She had never ex-pected to actually meet him, though. 'Is it for the wedding?'

'I wish it was,' Gary said ruefully. 'He'd be the ideal best man. No, he's here for a few weeks to look up old friends and have a holiday. He doesn't get many of those, not with the ranch in full swing. He should be here in a day or two. He rang from London. It's six years since he was last here.'

'And he hadn't changed much that I could see,' Mrs Hudson muttered, and Gary glanced at her irritably, no longer amused.

'Don't start on about Zade,' he snapped. 'He's just about perfect and you know it. He's not a boy any more. He's thirty-six and successful.'

'Good job,' his mother murmured, having her usual last word. 'He was trouble enough when he was a boy—a tearaway if ever I knew one. Dragged you into trouble often enough, that I know!'

'Dragged me out of it,' Gary corrected. He was sud-denly very grim-looking and even his mother knew to stop. They seemed to be talking about two different people, a villain and a saint. It would be interesting to meet this long-lost cousin, but Catrina hoped she would not be present if there were any arguments.

'Are you staying for supper, love?' Gary asked, but she was already standing to get her bag. Mrs Hudson was a bit more vitriolic than usual tonight and Catrina imagined it was because of the expected arrival of her nephew. She didn't much fancy facing this stealthy battle all evening.

'I can't, thanks. I only dropped in to give your mother a book she ordered. Dad's due in about now. He's got a stopover.'

'Funny job that, airline pilot,' Mrs Hudson sniffed. 'Here today and gone tomorrow. Don't know any other girl with a father who flies planes.'

She made it sound as if it wasn't quite respectable and Gary made a sour face behind her back.

'Maybe the other girls haven't got fathers with brains. Come on, Trina, I'll see you to your car.'

His mother looked as if she was going to point out that it was bitterly cold and that Catrina could see to herself, but she thought better of it and, in any case, she wanted something.

'Can you get me *Country Cooking*, Catrina?' she asked with one of her few smiles.

'It's in at the moment,' Catrina said thankfully. 'Somebody returned it tonight—you're lucky. It's a very popular book. I'll put it aside.'

'I'll keep it for the full time,' Gary's mother warned severely. 'I want to copy some recipes.'

Catrina nodded and said goodnight. Gary's mother filled her with gloom. It was just impossible to like her.

'Don't let her worry you,' Gary murmured as they left the kitchen and went to the door. 'I'll deal with her. She'll not be bossing my wife about.'

Catrina smiled up at him. She knew he meant it and so did his mother. This was a sort of last fling before she was deposed as lady of the house, but, even so, Catrina had a few qualms. With a mother-in-law like that next door, she would not be giving up her nice little job. It might prove to be a refuge.

It was icy-cold and she shivered, pulling her jacket close and fastening the zip. When the wind swept down the dale like this there was no knowing what the weather would do. She had never really become accustomed to the harsh winters here, the long, cold springs. Until she was eighteen she had lived in the much softer south.

'Go back inside, Gary,' she urged. 'I can get into my car without any help. You'll freeze.'

'I'm used to it,' he laughed, grabbing her arm and running her across the yard to the shelter of the barn, where her car stood. 'I'm damned if I'm missing my kiss.'

He pushed her back against the car and bent his fair head to search for her lips and Catrina lifted her head willingly. Gary did nothing to thrill her, but she loved him, and when she felt at all anxious about marriage she always reminded herself that she was just a bit odd. She had the dark eyes, the black, shining hair of her mother, but she had none of her mother's fiery, passionate Italian nature.

In fact, she never felt anything much. She felt loved and she knew Gary loved her as much as she loved him, but she also knew that the physical side of marriage would not be a necessity for her. She might have told her mother, but her mother was not there now; the flashing dark eyes had closed for the last time and there was nobody to discuss things with. She could hardly ask her father's advice and Mrs Hudson was not in any way motherly.

In any case, she knew that a lot of women felt like that. She had heard them talking quietly at the library and she had read a good many books. Mostly it was the man who felt the passion. Women often pretended.

Gary was feeling passion now, even though the wind was biting into them. He slid her zip down and felt urgently for her breast and Catrina couldn't help stiffening. Sometimes her own frigidity frightened her and she wondered if she should have let Gary rush her so swiftly into being engaged. She didn't really feel ready for marriage.

'Not here, Gary,' she managed quickly, and he raised his head and looked at her with slightly impatient eyes.

'Then where, Trina? I can guarantee that I'm the best-behaved fiancé in the dales. One day you'll have to soften up.'

'It's only nerves. I do love you, Gary.' She looked up at him and his tight expression relaxed as he smiled down at her.

'Into the car, you oddity,' he ordered with a grin. 'I'll have to deal with those nerves. On our wedding night you get two brandies.' He burst into laughter when she blushed and Catrina was glad to get into her small car and drive off. She had pushed the thought of the wedding night out of her mind for weeks and she did that determinedly now.

It was just nerves, wedding nerves. Most people probably felt like that. When she was married and settled down she would relax and not worry so much. She still missed her mother terribly and she was sure that had something to do with it. So much of the gaiety had gone out of her life.

The weather wasn't helping any, either. The leaden sky and bitter cold were depressing. It was nearly dark now and she forced herself to forget her problems. Her father might be home already and he would not want to see a gloomy face.

He was home. She drove back through the town and up into the hills at the other side and as she drew up by the cottage her headlights swung across his car and her heart lifted like magic. When he was away she sometimes felt as if she were backed into a corner with everything. She rushed in and he turned to grin at her as she tracked him down to the sitting-room.

'You're early!'

'A bit. I managed to get away straight off. No complications.' His clear eyes moved over her flushed cheeks and the shine of her tossing black curls. 'Had any complications yourself?'

'Only Gary's mother. I called to take her the book she ordered.'

'You should have conveniently forgotten,' he growled. 'I hope Gary was there to protect you?'

'Most of the time. Anyway, one does not forget things with Mrs Hudson. I'd never hear the last of it. She wants us to wait for the wedding until August now.'

'She's got the cheek of Old Harry!' he grunted, pouring himself a drink. 'I expect Gary set her right?'

'Of course. He got quite stroppy. It wasn't worth a battle, though. I wouldn't mind if she wanted to change it.'

Her father turned to look at her, frowning slightly as if he was trying to see into her head. Sometimes she seemed to be strung up tight, ready to snap and fall apart. Her cheerful looks didn't fool him. Since her mother's death she seemed to have drawn a tight shell around herself. The bright, easygoing Catrina had disappeared.

'Do you love him, Cat?'

'Of course! I'm marrying him.' She was surprised by the question, almost shocked, but she laughed up at him. He was a very big man, much taller than Gary. His brown, wavy hair was beginning to grey and in two years he would retire. She wasn't sure what he would do then, but he would be here, close to her, and that would be good.

'Do you sleep with him?' he persisted, and Catrina's face flushed. It was quite unexpected and not at all like her father.

'Of course not!' She turned away, but he reached across and tilted her face, looking down at her seriously.

'It would be normal, especially nowadays. You'll be married in two months.'

'Well, we're not married yet. I'll get your meal on.' She wanted to slide out of this unexpected conversation, but he was taking it all very matter-of-factly, as if it were quite normal. It reminded her that she was constantly asking herself if *she* was normal.

'No cooking. I'm taking you out. I booked at the Golden Calf.' It brightened her up and she turned to smile at him, glad to see the back of the unexpectedly personal discussion. Even though she was close to her father they never had this sort of conversation.

'Good! It's glamorous. Keep your uniform on; it makes me feel important.'

'You are important, Cat,' he assured her with a smile. 'You might soon be about as beautiful as your mother, but then I'm prejudiced. Maybe you're as beautiful right now.'

Like her, he had not in any way recovered from her mother's sudden death. They had met because of his job. Maria had been a stewardess and they had married very soon after meeting. Catrina had no other memories but happiness. There had been none of the bickering that she saw at Gary's house. Her mother and father seemed to have spent their lives with their arms around each other. There was now a great gap in their lives, but, for her, Gary filled the gap to some extent.

'Do you really want to marry him?' Her father had turned away as he always did when her mother was mentioned. He hid the grief, although she knew it was there.

'I love him.'

'Be sure, Cat,' he advised quietly. 'There are many kinds of love. Don't get them mixed up. I worry a bit.'

'You shouldn't.' She took his arm, hugging him, and he looked down at her steadily.

'Your mother and I couldn't keep away from each other. We slept together almost as soon as we met and it never dimmed. I want that for you, a magical life.'

'I haven't got my mother's fire,' she reminded him.

'Haven't you, love? I wonder.'

He let the matter drop and Catrina got ready to go out. He was wrong, of course. She was a mixture of them both. She had most of her mother's looks, but she had the steady ways of her father—the calm, even temper and the quick-thinking brain that made him one of the best pilots the airline had.

Fire was not part of her nature and it never would be. Funny he should have brought it up when she had been thinking about it herself. Somehow it had settled her mind. Comparing herself with her mother reminded her who she was, and she was not a beautiful, fiery creature who laughed, cried and made love with equal abandon. It had been what her father needed. She did not.

He was waiting for her at the bottom of the stairs when she came down and his eyes softened as he looked at her. Her crisp black hair was shining in the light, the short curls framing her face. Her dark eyes were softened, a warm brown that smiled and glowed. There was just the touch of Italian about her, but it was mainly the skin, faintly olive with apricot tinting her cheeks.

'You're beautiful,' her father said quietly. 'I hope Gary knows it. You want a bit more weight, though. I bet you don't eat when I'm not here.'

'I do,' Catrina laughed, taking his arm. 'To prove it, I'll have plenty tonight. Anyway, I'll be a farmer's wife soon. I'll be baking all day long.'

'Will you get the chance?' he asked wryly, opening the door for her.

'Maybe not. She says I'm not farming stock, born and bred.'

'Good God!' Her father gave a barking laugh and hurried her to his car and she settled back with a sigh. When he retired she would feel a bit more settled. He had met Mrs Hudson twice and each time he had looked her firmly in the eye and she had behaved herself. This cousin of Gary's would feel her displeasure. He would probably stay with them at the farm. What a way to spend a holiday!

It was a couple of days before she got to the farm again. Gary rang next day to say he had to be away at two markets, and she certainly didn't feel like going over to chat to his mother. In any case, her father was home for two whole days, and, as for the book, it could wait. She put it aside and told herself she would take it next time she went, although Gary's mother could easily have come for it.

When Gary came back he rang her and invited her for supper and Catrina hurried home to see her father off first. She always felt a little lost when he went, although she had had a lifetime to get used to it and he was very casual about his lifestyle, as if he were a bus driver.

'See you next weekend,' he called as he drove off, and Catrina went into the empty house. He would be in Bangkok by this time tomorrow, sleeping in some very good hotel and having a swim in the pool. She sometimes thought that was why Gary's mother objected so often. It all sounded just a bit too glamorous.

She put his things away carefully, ready for next time. The cottage was very nice, with its own huge garden. It stood at the end of the road that ran through the village and it was not some small country cottage either. At one time it had been, but various people had added extensions and now it was quite a big house. It seemed a big,

empty house without her mother, and Catrina got ready
to go for supper quickly. Every time her father left she
had this feeling of gloom, loneliness. It would take Gary
to cheer her out of it.

It was dark by the time she got there, still with that
bite in the air and as she parked her car Gary came out
to meet her, hugging her close. Even so, he didn't linger.
He hurried her to the house, away from the cold, and
as they stepped into the hall he pulled her to him again,
kissing her urgently, his mouth open over hers, and
Catrina submitted as usual, glad to see him, her heart
filled with affection. The talk with her father had done
her good because she knew herself a bit more. This
almost indifferent feeling was normal for her, but she
would have a happy marriage all the same. Many people
did who felt as she felt.

When he drew back he was breathing heavily and
Catrina felt just a bit embarrassed, as this was in the
house where his mother might appear with her disapproving face. He didn't usually push her that far and
she wondered if he had been thinking about his own
words, if he too was anxious about the wedding night.

She felt more than a bit embarrassed when she looked
up and saw the man who was watching with interest. He
was leaning against the door to the sitting-room, making
no attempt to draw back discreetly.

'Peeping Tom!' Gary said with a shout of laughter,
and vividly blue eyes narrowed with amusement.

'Just checking. I didn't know you had it in you.' The
brilliant eyes ran over Catrina like blue fire and the firm
lips twisted in a smile. 'Still, on second thoughts I can
understand. So this is my new cousin?'

'Almost,' Gary said happily, and Catrina stood like
stone, a funny, defenceless wave sweeping over her. She
had a feeling of dropping to pieces and an even more
frightening urge to just run. The blue eyes watched her

steadily, not letting her escape. They dominated her with a sort of dazzling command.

She had the terrible thought now that Gary had shown so much passion deliberately, knowing that this man would be watching, but she pushed the idea aside. Why should he? He had nothing to prove.

'This is Zade,' Gary said proudly, but she had already fathomed that one out. Zade Mackensie had arrived and he was not a man to be easily dismissed. There was something about him that made Gary's mother fade to the very back of Catrina's mind.

'Can she talk?' The deep voice was edged with a transatlantic accent and Catrina realised she had just been staring. He straightened from the doorway and she got more of a shock. He was taller than her father, lean, hard and quite alarming, towering over both of them. Those eyes were so brilliantly blue that they held the attention and she only just noticed how tanned he was, how tough-looking, not an ounce of spare flesh on him. Suddenly she knew why Mrs Hudson didn't like this man. He was untouchable, almost dangerous. His eyes were astonishing and they had never even glanced away from her.

'Say something, Trina.' Gary laughed, looking at her in amusement, and she made a great effort to be normal, going forward, her hand held out.

'Hello Mr Mackensie. I'm Catrina Arnold.'

'Catrina?' He took her hand and his own hand just about swallowed it as he looked down at her intently and odd shivers ran right up her arm. 'An exotic name. Did you make it up?'

She blinked at the unexpected question, not knowing how to answer, and Gary grinned at them both as Zade looked down at her with scientific interest. He made no move to release her hand. She had meant this to be a handshake, but he had merely taken her hand and held it.

'You'll get used to him, Trina. He just says whatever he thinks.'

Oh, no, he didn't! He had complete control of his mind and his tongue and he was laughing at her, not outright, but deep inside.

'I didn't!' She snatched her hand away, finding it difficult not to glare in self-defence. 'My mother was Italian.'

'That explains the colouring.' He was still inspecting her wryly and she knew he found her definitely wanting as a bride for his beloved cousin. It was difficult to be normal when he seemed to be looking right through her.

'Trina's father is an airline pilot,' Gary explained. 'He's just gone off this afternoon. Where is it this time, love?'

'Bangkok,' she managed briefly. It was getting a bit difficult to breathe. She didn't know if it was anger or astonishment and she began to struggle out of her coat, grateful to have the excuse to move.

Zade Mackensie leaned back against the door as Gary's mother called sharply from the kitchen and Gary went with a rueful glance to see what she wanted. It gave Catrina a feeling of panic to be left and she silently berated herself. It was only because this man was different, not like anyone she had ever seen. All the same, she had an instinctive desire to fight him off, to tell him to stop looking at her. The urge to walk out of the door was very strong.

'Do you ever go with your father?' he asked, with not a lot of interest.

'You mean so he can look after me?' Catrina spun round and snapped at him and she was instantly ashamed of herself. She didn't know what had got into her and dark eyebrows rose at her tone.

'Cat by name and cat by nature,' he murmured, straightening up again. 'Come along. I'll find you a drink, because my aunt is never going to offer one, although she may have the odd drop of hemlock put aside. That will be for me, of course. I expect you can have a sherry.'

He took her arm, drawing her into the warmth of the sitting-room. He was awful, domineering, arrogant and utterly without warmth. He was here to see Gary and nothing more. He had his aunt summed up and she could tell that he didn't care one way or the other. Gary just happened to be his long-time protégé, otherwise he wouldn't be here.

When he handed her a drink she was at great pains to make sure their fingers didn't touch and she also kept her head averted, refusing to make any effort to speak. She was well aware that it was childish, but his presence was so dominant that it was either fight, run or hide.

He sat opposite, his legs stretched out, the chair tilted back on its legs at a dangerous angle. What Gary's mother would say to that Catrina didn't like to think. Probably nothing at all, though. He was not a man who would calmly allow reprimands, and Catrina had the feeling that one steely look would quell even Mrs Hudson.

When she looked up he was watching her, his eyes narrowed and amused on her face.

'Are you old enough to get married?' He had this devastating way of looking, probing and coming straight to the point, and she knew she must seem a bit odd. Nobody had ever had this effect on her.

'I'm twenty-four, Mr Mackensie,' she said stiffly. He just nodded and went on staring at her, ignoring her starchy attitude.

'Gary says you're a librarian.'

'In town. It's only a small library.' She just murmured the words, annoyed at the cross-examination, and he suddenly grinned, white teeth flashing against his tanned face.

'Never talk yourself down, Catrina,' he advised ironically. 'You'll have to get over that if you're to tackle my aunt. You'll need to be tough.'

His aunt came in then, looking at them suspiciously, and Catrina was almost glad to see her—anything to get out of this situation.

'Can I help?' she asked hopefully, but Mrs Hudson shook her head and turned back to the kitchen, her lips set tight. 'Just sit at the table. Gary helped. I'll serve.'

'Well, I assume that means me too,' Zade said drily. He stood and looked sardonically at Catrina. 'Come along, Miss Arnold, you and I are guests.'

'Are you staying here at the farm?' she asked, desperately trying to be normal and seek some sort of conversation as he held her chair for her.

'Ah! You make jokes? A young lady with wit.' He gave her a wry glance as he sat down. 'I'm staying at the Golden Calf. I'm not my aunt's best friend, as you no doubt know. I'm here to see Gary and observe his future wife. My aunt is a necessary obstacle.'

It really was a very awkward meal. At least it was for Catrina. She found it difficult to speak and, as far as she could remember afterwards, Mrs Hudson simply sat there and ate with no conversation at all. Zade and Gary talked endlessly, but Catrina was too tightened up to hear anything. She would not have eaten except that Zade kept passing food to her and she automatically put it on her plate.

Both Gary and his cousin behaved as if there were no atmosphere at all, and they would not have noticed if she hadn't been there. In short, it was a man's evening. They didn't need either Catrina or Gary's mother.

When she pleaded tiredness and got up to go, Zade got up too.

'Oh, you don't have to leave, do you, Zade?' Gary looked very disappointed, much more disappointed than he had looked at the idea of Catrina going.

'Sorry, I do. I'm tired too.' Zade smiled apologetically. 'I'll probably see you tomorrow. There are people I want to see, places I want to go, but I'll be around for a while.'

'Long enough for the wedding?' Gary wheedled, but he got a very definite shake of the head.

'No way. I have to get back long before then. Bart's retired. He's just holding the fort for a few weeks. I can't leave him for long.'

When they went outside Catrina soon sidled up to her car, getting away from them as they stood talking. The whole evening had shaken her and she wanted to get away fast. Zade Mackensie upset her and she wasn't quite sure why. Well, it was all over now. She was thankful he wasn't staying for the wedding. It would have given a new meaning to bridal nerves.

She would start the car to let them know she was leaving. They looked as if they were going to stand in the cold and talk all night long and she was clearly superfluous to requirements.

She tried, but when she turned the key nothing at all happened except a small, miserable noise. It gained their attention, though, and when she tried again they both sauntered across.

'What's wrong?' Gary asked, and she felt quite cross. It was not her fault, but no doubt Zade Mackensie would smile that sardonic smile and ask if she could drive. He was back to watching her and now he was definitely amused again.

'It won't start.' She just knew what was coming next.

'Move over. I'll have a go,' Gary got in and normally she would have been grateful, but she had enough mechanical knowledge to know that it was a waste of time.

'Flat battery,' Gary announced.

'How can it be?' Catrina asked impatiently. 'I didn't leave any lights on. It got me here.'

'That's true, love, but it's not going to get you back. I'll have to take you.'

Catrina's relief was short-lived.

'Don't bother, I'll take her. I have to get back to the hotel and that's just out of town.'

'I'll take a taxi!' The idea of riding with him was just too much, but they both looked at her as if she were mad, and finally she found herself going to Zade's car, waving goodbye to Gary. However irritated she felt, there was nothing she could do about it.

It was dark in the car and Catrina shivered. He had bothered her all evening and now she was enclosed here with him. It wasn't just the cold that made her feel shivery. He turned the heating up and the fan blasted warm air at her and she sank lower into her seat.

'How will you get to work tomorrow?' It forced her into reluctant speech.

'I'll get a taxi. I could have got a taxi now quite well.'

'With a fiancé and a near-cousin standing by? What a self-reliant girl you are, Catrina. Or is it just irritation?' His remarks silenced her and she didn't speak again. She was much too aware of him. Too aware that he was big, powerful and in control. Too aware that he was sitting beside her. Too aware that the hands on the steering-wheel were strong, efficient and alarming. It was irritation. She didn't like Zade Mackensie and it was useless to pretend otherwise.

CHAPTER TWO

'WHERE do you live?' Zade's question forced her into speech and she told him briefly. He nodded, looking straight ahead. 'I remember that place. It used to be a little cottage, but some city man bought it and extended it. Pity.'

'It's not a pity!' Catrina said with more heat than necessary. 'It's a very comfortable house. Victorian times are gone. Anyway, we didn't do it. We've only been here six years.'

'I know. I was over here at the time. I remember the interest in the new arrivals.'

'I don't remember you,' Catrina said sharply, astonished that she hadn't picked up some warning signal of vexation if he had been anywhere near.

'Well, I didn't lean over the gate and watch you cart in the furniture,' he acknowledged wryly. 'Why are you so edgy?' he added softly. 'Or is it just me?'

'I'm not edgy,' Catrina began stormily and then stopped, biting at her lip. She was well on the way to making a fool of herself. 'Well, if you must know, I was expecting trouble all evening.'

'And you don't like trouble?'

'I'm not used to it. In any case, who does?'

'At one time it followed me around. My aunt remembers in bright detail. I think that was the trouble you sensed.' He gave a grunt of impatience and she risked a look at his strong profile. He wasn't a bit like Gary. He was hard and his humour was definitely of the sarcastic type. All the same, she risked conversation and even a question.

'Why doesn't she like you? After all, she's family.'

'I don't think she believes that,' Zade said quietly. 'My father was her brother and she clung to him as she clings to Gary. When he died she expected to take over his authority, although not his responsibility. My mother was still young and she married again.'

'The man you call Bart?'

'Sure.' She almost saw the smile that lit his face. 'Bart is a great guy. He took us both off to the States and adopted me officially. Now I run the ranch myself—with the odd amount of interference.'

'Wasn't Gary's mother glad to see you getting on in the world?' Catrina asked, and he shot a glance at her that was utterly sardonic.

'No. She hadn't planned it. You're taking on a handful there, little girl.'

'I'm not a little girl,' Catrina pointed out. 'I'm getting married in two months' time.'

'I hope she lets you,' he drawled wryly. 'I'm still paying for the trouble I got Gary into twenty years ago.'

'Gary says you got him out of trouble, not into it. Why have you come when you're not welcome?'

'I come back from time to time. Just to look around. I like to see Gary, anyway. She doesn't bother me.'

'But you're staying at the Golden Calf.' Catrina had quite forgotten whom she was talking to and, at this gleeful little dig, he slanted her a brilliant look that silenced her.

'I like a free hand. There's not much entertainment at the farm.'

'There's not much entertainment of that type in town either,' Catrina snapped back, wishing she had kept quiet. She had walked right into that one.

'You know about such things?' he asked softly. 'I thought little girls went to bed early? Or did you just read it in the library?'

His goading comment made her hotter than ever and she sat like a stone until she felt as if every bone were ready to snap. She was determined not to speak again. This was somebody she had only just met. He was also Gary's cousin; she should have been chatting to him comfortably. People didn't usually bother her much, but he bothered her. He seemed to be filling the air with a sort of power, a vibrancy she had never known with anyone. She had felt it as soon as she had seen him and here, in the car, so close to him, it was choking her. She had never disliked anyone so much.

It was with great joy that she saw her own house and signalled him to stop at the gate.

'It's pitch-black,' he muttered, bending and peering at the house. 'This is a lonely place, right at the end of the road. I'm surprised your father leaves you alone.'

'What do you suggest he does with me? I'm not a teenager, Mr Mackensie. I can take care of myself,' Catrina snapped, her annoyance boiling over. 'We both have our jobs. My father just happens to be away a lot.'

He switched on the interior light, draped his arm along the back of the seat, and turned to look at her.

'Bring Gary over here at night,' he said seriously, as if the idea should have occurred to her. 'I'm not about to suggest you move in at the farm, of course. I'm not a sadist. Aunty would eat you.' Back to sarcasm, he looked at her with a wry grin, and she felt heat flood into her face.

'Gary and I are not married yet.'

He just gazed at her in silence, his startling eyes searching her face, and then his brows drew together in a frown.

'I'm not exactly sure I heard that,' he said quietly. 'You're engaged.'

'I can't see what that's got to do with it,' Catrina said crossly, wondering how she had got into this intimate and embarrassing conversation, why he had put the light on, and why he was at all interested in her affairs.

'Are you certain you love my cousin, Miss Arnold?' he asked in a quiet voice, and she could quite see then why he had come all the way from America to inspect her. He had to make quite sure that Gary was not making a mistake. Not only was he treating her like an idiot, he was treating Gary like a child.

'Quite certain, and even if I didn't it would be none of your business!'

'I'll be damned!' he murmured softly. He switched off the light and leaned back, gazing at the mist through the windscreen. 'I thought girls like you were extinct. Go inside before the fairies claim you. I'll stay until you get some lights on.'

'There's no need!' Catrina seethed, getting out of the car and standing with the door open to glare down at him. 'I don't need you to guard me and I don't need your sarcastic, personal remarks either.' He just ignored her temper, settling back to watch her to the door and obviously not about to move off until he was satisfied. He didn't even bother to look at her.

'I'll decide about guarding. When I brought you home I took responsibility for you. It's not going to be my fault if anything happens to the last surviving virgin.'

Catrina turned and ran up the path, not caring if she fell. She slammed the front door even though the house was dark, but the car didn't leave until she had all the downstairs lights on.

What a night! She felt a twinge of sympathy for Mrs Hudson. Zade Mackensie was impossible. It probably took the whole of the United States to contain him. She hoped he would go soon, because she certainly didn't want to meet him again. He infuriated her.

She had a shower and brushed her short black curls vigorously, still seething with annoyance. Just who did he think he was, speaking to her like that? She couldn't even tell Gary. Somehow it had been much too intimate, and she flushed again with shame when she remembered the things he had said. He had attacked her right from the start.

Not that Gary had noticed. He was too wrapped up in his dashing cousin. If she had been sitting looking at an empty plate all evening nobody would have seen. She grimaced when she remembered that Zade had seen. He had simply kept on talking, but, thinking it over, she realised that he seemed to have kept an eye on her. He had things in her hands almost before she knew she wanted them herself. He probably thought she was too slender for Gary.

She snorted with annoyance and got into bed. One good thing had happened: Mrs Hudson had been utterly silent. She looked as if she really hated Zade. Well, he would be gone soon, and Gary's mother would finally calm down. She would also calm down herself. It was lucky Zade Mackensie didn't still live in town. He would be interfering all the time and she could just imagine that Gary would agree with everything his powerful cousin said.

Next day was Catrina's half-day. She took a taxi to work and was home by one o'clock. When she rang the garage they said the car wouldn't be ready until the next day.

As she put the phone down, Gary rang, and he was bubbling with excitement.

'Come right over, Trina. I've got a great surprise.'

She smiled at this enthusiasm, but reminded him she had no car as yet. Apparently that was no drawback.

'I'll fetch you,' he said quickly. 'Wrap up warm; we'll be outside.' He would allow no further questions and Catrina went straight away to change. She knew him. When he had some great enthusiasm he rushed around like a boy. By the time he arrived she was wearing jeans, her red anorak and a white woolly cap. She was well aware that it was cold and out at the farm it would be bitter. Gary's enthusiasm often lasted a long time.

No questions were allowed. He was just grinning and she was to wait and see. Catrina smiled to herself. After a dose of Zade Mackensie last night she felt very indulgent towards Gary.

'We've got to get back before Zade arrives,' he muttered, driving fast. 'I want to see his surprise. This is going to stop him in his tracks.'

Catrina's face fell, her interest dying at once. Zade Mackensie was going to be there. She hadn't forgotten last night. It had coloured her whole morning, almost making her snappy at work. Now she had to face him again, and so soon! She wished she had known, because she certainly wouldn't have come.

The thought made her feel a touch of guilt. It really was not nice of her to be like this. Gary rarely saw his cousin and she only had to be pleasant for a little while, then he would be back in whatever place he came from and out of her sight. If she was prepared to put up with Gary's mother, why couldn't she just put up with his cousin too? This time she would try, and she would try to ignore his sarcasm. It would be possible if she pretended he was just a rare visitor.

The surprise was quite a shock. Gary drove into the yard and then took her over to the near paddock, dragging her along, grinning all over his face.

'There!' he pronounced, pointing across the windswept field, and Catrina couldn't really think of a suitable comment. The surprise was a big one, she had to admit.

It was a horse, a chestnut, and it was not looking too enthusiastic about its surroundings as far as she could tell.

'It—it's beautiful,' she commented. 'Where did it come from?' He burst into laughter and hugged her.

'Love, you're a scream! You sound as if you think it just wandered in. I wish Zade could have heard that. I *bought* the great beast!'

Catrina had assumed as much. Her rather odd remark had been because she had no idea at all what to say. She knew almost for certain that Gary could not ride, and both he and his mother had made so many remarks about the people near by who did ride that Catrina couldn't believe she was actually seeing a horse on their land.

All she could do was watch it, standing by the fence and glad of the woolly hat. Gary was too excited to be cold, and when he heard a car he turned and went back to the yard.

'Wait here,' he ordered. 'That's Zade.'

Catrina was really too cold to wait there, but she certainly didn't want to go to greet Zade Mackensie. Now that he was arriving her good resolutions were fading away fast. No doubt he would also enthuse over the horse and she would have to either stand and freeze or go into the house and encounter Gary's mother. She didn't know which idea she hated most.

Zade was wearing a thick jacket. He didn't look cold at all. He had it open, his hands pushed into the pockets, and he didn't seem to mind the wind blasting at him, although he only had a thin black sweater between him and the bitter cold.

He didn't look at all enthusiastic either. He nodded at her and then ignored her, his eyes on the horse, and Catrina saw his mouth set in one tight line of disapproval.

'What do you think?' Gary asked, still excited.

'About what?' Zade just stared across the field grimly and Gary's face slipped slightly from his beaming smile.

'The horse! Damn it all, Zade. You're the expert. Is it a good buy? I just told you how much I paid. Get a close look, can't you?'

'Can't *you*?' Zade asked drily.

'Not without chasing all over to catch it.' Gary sounded just a little peeved and Catrina looked from one to the other, sensing an atmosphere, but not understanding it. 'We can walk round the field and it will probably stand still.'

'Not if it's got any sense,' Zade bit out. 'It's too bloody cold for a horse to be out. It's not a working horse. That one's used to warm stabling. You haven't even got a blanket on it. I hope it's insured, because leave it there for much longer and you're back to the Land Rover.'

'I only left it out to give you a glimpse,' Gary began defensively, and Zade shot him a look of utter exasperation.

'Right. I'll have a glimpse.' He went up to the fence and gave a sharp, piercing whistle, and the animal turned, walked towards them, and then broke into a canter. In seconds it was standing looking at Zade intelligently, and Gary gave a quick laugh.

'You'll have to teach me that.'

'And a lot more,' Zade muttered, climbing the fence and walking round the horse, feeling its legs and looking into its impassive face. 'It's a good one. Not a bargain, but OK.'

'What did I tell you?' Gary said to Catrina, excited again.

'Get it under cover now!' Zade ordered, climbing back and dusting himself off.

'Well, I haven't got a place quite ready yet...' Gary began, and, to Catrina's astonishment, Zade turned on him with blazing eyes.

'Then put it on the settee and tell your mother to stay in the kitchen! This animal is uncomfortable. It's soft, and I'm beginning to have my doubts about you too!'

Catrina was stunned. She didn't know what to do at all. She felt she should be siding with Gary and getting annoyed, but deep down she knew that Zade was right. Gary went slightly red, but he just laughed it off.

'I'll put it in the barn for now.'

It had to be Zade who led it out of the field, though, and Zade who wrapped his hand in the thick mane and brought it across to the barn.

'What the hell do you want with a horse?' he suddenly snapped. 'You've never ridden in your life.'

'I'm going to learn,' Gary said stubbornly. 'Catrina can learn on it as well.'

'*It*,' Zade bit out, 'is a stallion. If you keep on trying like this you'll have no horse and no wife. When it's not blue with cold it will have a mind of its own. This is not a mount for a woman. It's not a mount for a learner, either. And why you've developed this taste for equestrian skills I'll never know.'

'You ride!' Gary said huffily, close to temper, but keeping it down, and Catrina had to admit he had good cause for temper. Zade was taking him apart.

'I work on horseback,' Zade pointed out irritably. 'There are plenty of places on the ranch that a pick-up can't get to. I also fly a helicopter. You fancy one of those too?'

Gary just took the horse and went into the barn and Zade snorted angrily, walking away as if he was only just keeping his rage bottled up.

'Don't learn on that horse!' He suddenly spun round and glared at Catrina. 'It will put you in hospital.'

'I wouldn't think of it,' she said calmly. 'As a matter of fact, I can ride.'

'Of course,' he sneered. 'The daughter of an airline pilot. Status.'

'Schoolgirl enthusiasm,' she corrected crossly. 'And don't think you're taking your temper out on me, Mr Mackensie. I'm not your cousin. If Gary wants to take that and keep quiet it's his business, but I won't take it!'

'All right. All right.' He suddenly grinned at her, charming and amused. 'So I'm a bad-tempered bastard. Schoolboy enthusiasm irritates me. Come on. It's too cold here for you. Let's go into the house. I'm in a good mood for Aunty. I'm just about ready to put her in the barn too.'

Catrina found herself smiling and he took her arm, hurrying her along.

'Gary never has a spare minute. I can't think why he wants a horse,' she mused thoughtlessly.

He stopped and looked down at her.

'Can't you? I assumed you were bright. If you can't figure that out, you're sadly lacking.'

He didn't say anything else, but he went on looking at her, and Catrina figured it out. Hero-worship. Gary wanted to be like Zade.

'There's nothing wrong with admiring somebody,' she pointed out in Gary's defence.

'Maybe not,' he acceded quietly, 'but copying their habits is something to grow out of.'

'You should be pleased he admires you,' Catrina said in a reprimanding voice. 'I can't see any reason to hurt his feelings.'

'I'm more concerned about the horse,' Zade said shortly. 'I can live without admiration.'

'Which is probably a good thing,' Catrina said tartly. The brilliant eyes ran over her in amusement, his mouth tilting in laughter.

'Oh, I do realise I haven't touched your heart, my lady,' he said softly. 'I think we could call it fight on sight.'

He stood smiling down at her and Catrina blushed furiously, not knowing what to say. He took her arm and continued towards the house, still smiling to himself.

'Let's get you indoors,' he suggested. 'Your face is the colour of your jacket. So much brilliance is blinding. Don't worry about not liking me. I'll survive it.'

Catrina bit her lips together in renewed annoyance. She was sure he would survive it. His only concern had been for the horse. It probably explained his attitude well. He was not too keen on people; horses came first, or maybe cattle. Women would be right at the end of the line.

Gary's mother came to see who was there and then very rapidly vanished. It made Catrina feel most uncomfortable and, now that they were indoors, more or less alone, and her temper had gone, Zade made her feel uncomfortable too. His taunting eyes seemed to be on her all the time and she didn't know where to look.

Mrs Hudson went so far as to make them a tray of tea and they were just drinking it, getting warm, when Gary came back in. His temper too was under control and Catrina suspected that the reason for that was because Zade had the most cutting tongue in the universe.

She was now wanting to go home, but hesitated to mention it. She had no car and she didn't want a repetition of last night. Gary's mother settled it all. There was the sound of a car in the yard and she came out dressed for the outside, pulling her gloves on and looking decidedly smug.

'Well, that's my lift,' she said almost gleefully. 'You can cook supper tonight, Catrina. It will give you a bit of practice. It's my WI night.'

Catrina was stunned, not because she couldn't cook, but because Gary's mother was letting her loose in the kitchen. It was obviously a well-thought-out ploy and she didn't want to stay here anyway, not with Zade here.

'We're going out to eat,' Gary announced before she could speak. 'I've booked for three at the Red Lion. It's a new place out on the Sellerby road,' he added, turning to Zade. 'Plenty of lights and music. Good food.'

Catrina looked startled. She had never been there with Gary. It was all news to her. He caught her glance and grinned.

'Merely hearsay,' he told her. 'I've booked for seven-thirty.'

It didn't leave a lot of time as she had to get changed and, as his mother went off, Catrina turned back to Gary.

'I'll need to get changed, then.'

'Can't you go like that, love? You look very nice. Red suits you.'

Catrina looked at him in amazement. She was wearing jeans and she felt very untidy.

'Gary! I can't go out to dinner like this!'

'I've got a lot to do,' he murmured seriously, and Zade stood up and looked down at them.

'That you have,' he agreed. 'I hope you're not going to let that horse just wander around the barn all night. I'll take Catrina.'

'Honestly, love, I was just joking,' Gary said, grinning at her and leaning across to give her a hug.

'So long as you're not joking about the work,' Zade interrupted sardonically. 'I'll take her, however. I have to change too. I'll drop her off and pick her up on the way back.'

She couldn't refuse. Once again she was with Zade, like it or not, and Gary didn't look too enthusiastic about the horse now. She could understand why. He always had a lot of jobs to do at night. Now he had taken on even more and, while Zade was here, the horse would get top priority.

Zade dropped her off and was back exactly on time to pick her up. He made her feel strange, and uneasy. Somehow he had come between her and Gary. Without saying anything at all he was there, separating them. It wasn't just his presence, either. It was his attitude, and she couldn't quite put her finger on it.

The Red Lion was one of those new road-houses that Catrina did not particularly care for. The lights were too bright and so was the company. The place seemed to be filled with young people all talking at once and Catrina noticed Zade's dark brows rise in impatience. They did have something in common, because he didn't like it either.

As Gary took her coat and settled her in her seat, her eyes met Zade's, and he looked back at her steadily. There was nothing taunting about him at the moment. There was just the steady appraisal, and it was a bit like drowning in the sky. In the light those brilliant eyes were piercingly blue, assessing, questioning, and she assumed that he was wondering how she would be as a wife for Gary. She wasn't surprised. He seemed to have Gary right under his thumb.

Her cheeks flushed and she was glad that Gary was taking so long to put her coat away.

'Will I do, Mr Mackensie?' she asked sharply, driven to saying something. She wished she hadn't. His eyes moved, running over her, lingering on the slender poise of her neck, her smooth shoulders and the high tilt of her breasts.

'You'll do beautifully, Miss Arnold,' he said softly. 'For what, is an entirely different matter.'

Catrina looked down at once. She had really asked for that. She should know better by now than to challenge Zade. Even Gary didn't challenge him. Her defiance had brought his derision back immediately and she knew what he meant.

She had taken a great deal of trouble tonight. She was carefully made up, and her dress was close-fitting, peach silk, the skirt swirling around her calves. It was off the shoulder, just enough to make it dressy, and she knew it was a little too much for this place, a little too cool for the weather, as the coat was silk too. It was silly to have worn it, but she had felt the need to put on a front with Zade there. All she had done was give him the chance to sum her up further.

She felt like clinging to Gary when he came back. She wanted to show Zade how close they were. She wanted to cut Zade out because he was some sort of danger. Instead she just went very quiet, but Gary didn't seem to notice. He liked it here.

After the meal Gary wanted to stay. He was enjoying himself, and as they had all come in Zade's car it was impossible to break up the party. Catrina had to dance whether she wanted to or not and she had never felt quite so uncomfortable in her life. She told herself that Gary did not often get out like this, but, all the same, it was a strain.

On the way back to the table he was stopped by a woman Catrina had never seen before and, as Catrina sank to her seat, Gary was dragged to another party, where people stood around laughing and talking.

'Which seems to leave you and me,' Zade murmured, looking across at her. 'I can see that Gary is as popular as ever.'

'He's very nice. Why shouldn't he be popular?'

'You feel the need to defend him? Don't forget I'm on his side too—cousinly affection. What else do you imagine brings me here?'

'I'm sorry,' Catrina said almost in a whisper. She was feeling very lost and when loud laughter had them both raising their heads she was even more dismayed. The woman was clinging to Gary's arm, laughing up at him, and Catrina couldn't help comparing the woman with herself. There was something voluptuous about her. Her curvy figure spoke louder than words. She would have no marriage problems, no secret fears. She looked sensuous and Gary looked just a little excited.

'Dance!' Zade ordered abruptly and gave her no chance to refuse. He was standing and drawing her to her feet almost before she had time to think. Before anxiety could take hold she was in his arms, swept on to the floor and lost in the noisy crowd. He just danced around with her, shielding her from knocks as a few novice dancers collided with them.

'Fun!' Zade muttered sarcastically. 'Just what I needed.'

'If we had come in two cars you could have——'

'Walked off and left you to it,' he finished for her, drawing back and looking down at her. 'Well, Catrina, I could do that now, couldn't I? There are plenty of taxis. You want me to walk out and leave you?'

She didn't answer. She didn't want him to go. If he went she would be sitting there all alone until Gary chose to come back. She automatically defended him in her mind. If she had been just with Gary he would not have gone off and left her. But she wasn't too sure and she didn't try to defend him aloud.

It was clear later on that Gary had had a little too much to drink and when they left Zade put him firmly in the back of the car, keeping Catrina in the front. It had been a miserable day and a miserable evening and for once Catrina couldn't blame Zade. She knew just how he felt.

He deposited Gary at home and then drove off with her, refusing coffee and advising Gary to go to bed. It was quite late and Catrina was shivering with cold. She didn't want the goodnight kiss Gary insisted on bestowing. She was feeling raw and Zade's presence was embarrassing her.

He almost bundled Gary into the house and as they walked back to the car Catrina saw a very tight look on Zade's face. Gary had not only ruined her evening, but he had forced Zade to stay in a place he didn't like. It had not been a good day for Zade either.

He glanced down at her and took off his jacket, draping it around her shoulders, and she was instantly jumpy.

'I'm all right, thank you!' she said quickly. He was now in his shirt-sleeves and not looking at all concerned about that.

'You're not. You're frozen. Don't worry, Catrina, I'm a very healthy specimen,' he murmured. 'You'll not catch anything, although a little common sense might just get through to you.'

She wasn't worried about catching anything. She felt surrounded. His jacket was warm, the heat of his skin still on it. It had picked up the scent of his aftershave and she wanted to take it off and climb into the back of the car, as far away from him as possible.

It was a very easy time at the library next day. The cold was keeping people away and Catrina had the chance to catch up on a few sorting-out jobs. She felt a sharp jolt as she came upon the book Gary's mother had ordered. It should have been taken over already, but she had forgotten. Well, if Gary's mother wanted it she could come and get it, because until Zade went it was best to keep away. Every instinct told her that clearly.

A glance at her watch showed it was almost time to close for lunch and she stayed at the front desk, trying to finish off before she left, frowning but not looking up as the door opened and another person came in. It would delay her and today she really needed her lunch break.

'*Country Cooking*, please.' The dark, goading voice had Catrina jumping, hoping she was dreaming, but teasing blue eyes looked down at her as Zade stood there by the desk. She just refused to acknowledge that her legs had turned to jelly.

'Sorry. It's ordered.' She forced herself to look back at him pertly and he grinned, his eyes flaring with amusement.

'You forgot to bring it. Bad girl. Your name is now mud.'

Catrina found herself smiling as she put the book out for him. Last night seemed to have been forgotten. It was somehow quite normal to see him.

'Are you trying to get round her?' she asked drily.

'I never go for the impossible. This is a Christian act, ma'am. It also gave me a good excuse to get out of there. Gary was otherwise engaged.' He looked round the library with interest. 'This place is still the same. Quaint.'

'I suppose they have nothing but the best in America?' Catrina asked, glancing at the time. She pressed the bell on the desk and raised her voice. 'The library is now closing until two o'clock,' she announced firmly.

'Power and authority,' Zade murmured, his lips quirking. 'That's why you like to work here.'

People were bringing their books to be checked out and Catrina was kept busy for a while, but she was stunningly aware that Zade still lounged by the desk, making no move to go. When the last person left she busily cleared up, suddenly too shy to speak.

'Going for lunch?' Zade asked quietly. She nodded and he went on, 'Do you go home?'

'No. It's a bit too far and I wouldn't get a good break by the time I'd made something to eat. In any case, I haven't got my car yet.'

'The garage will deliver it here at four,' he informed her. 'That's the message from Gary. So where do you go for lunch?'

'There's a tea-shop just opposite,' Catrina said breathlessly, glancing up. Quite suddenly, she realised she didn't want him to go away, and he looked down at her steadily for a second, holding her eyes with ease, looking at her for a lot longer than she wanted.

'I don't fancy it,' he said softly. 'We'll go to the Golden Calf.'

'But—but I——'

'But you what?' He took her arm and urged her to the door. 'Are you scared to be seen with your future cousin? Aunty is baking bread. Who else cares?'

'It—it wasn't that.' Catrina knew her cheeks were flushed and she knew she was shivering inside almost uncontrollably, but she was being steadily impelled to the door all the same.

'I'm paying. So what other excuse can you think of? Be quick. I've got a lousy temper and you know it.' When she glanced up he was grinning down at her and she just gave in, gladly getting into his car out of the sudden blast of cold air and snuggling into the warmth.

'I've had the heating going all the way here just for you,' he said. 'You seem to feel the cold so I thought I'd better prepare.'

'How did you know I'd agree to come to lunch?'

'Well, first I had to find out if you were still scared of me, and as you seemed to be reasonably in control of your terrors and your bursts of temper I figured it would be worth the risk of asking you.'

'I'm not scared of you,' Catrina protested.

'Aren't you? So what is it, then?' He looked across at her, pinning her with blue eyes that probed almost painfully, and she felt her breath tighten as she struggled to look away.

'Maybe I don't like you.' It was supposed to be an amusing bit of bravado, but it came out in a very trembling manner, and he just went on looking at her steadily, not starting the car. When she suddenly dropped her head he turned away, driving off up the street, and it was terrible that he didn't say anything—no sarcasm, no goading, no jokes.

'I'm sorry,' she blurted out, and he just went on driving, his eyes on the road.

'Sorry you don't like me or sorry that you're lying?' he asked softly. 'This is a friendly gesture, Catrina. I'm at a loose end and I thought it a good idea to get to know Gary's future wife a little better. I'm not stalking you.'

'I never thought you were stalking me and I was only... I've changed my mind about lunch. Can I get out, please?' Catrina asked urgently.

'No, you can't! We're on our way. I'm not about to eat you. I'll order something more substantial.'

It was a great relief to hear him back to sarcasm and Catrina sat silently, her cheeks burning, and no amount of trying would stop the shaking. He frightened her without any stalking and it was something inside her. Her hands gripped together when she asked herself why. Why did he frighten her? Why did he have this effect on her? Why had she started trembling from the first moment she had seen him? She just couldn't speak at all and Zade didn't even try.

CHAPTER THREE

ZADE spoke when they pulled into the car park of the hotel.

'This place is good, comfortable. Do you come here with Gary?'

'No. My father brings me here for a meal when he's home. We try to get out at least once each time he's here and we like the quiet of this place.'

She was on safe ground with her father and they went inside, Zade grimacing as the heat hit them. She had noticed the way they kept the heat up in here and clearly Zade found it uncomfortable. He took off his jacket and helped her off with her coat. She was wearing a suit because it was not too warm in the library and he nodded at the jacket.

'Want that off too? You're going to boil.'

It seemed silly to refuse, although she would have liked to. She didn't want him to look at her and she knew it was sheer nonsense. She had asked for that look last night. When she slid out of the jacket and stood feeling slender and defenceless in her suit skirt and black sweater he didn't even glance at her. His eyes were on the waiter who hurried over and led them to a table at the side of the room.

Zade didn't take a lot of notice of her then either. He was ordering for them and when she had chosen she had the chance to watch him as he spoke to the waiter. She saw how broad his shoulders were, how strong he looked, his muscles clear under the fine white sweater. His hair was dark brown, crisp and shining, and anyone could tell he spent a lot of time out of doors. The tan was deep and smooth, making his astonishing eyes more brilliantly blue. They looked as if they could see a long way.

She was still studying him as he looked up, dismissing the waiter and giving her his undivided, worrying attention.

'So now what?' he asked quizzically.

'I was just wondering about you,' she said, and he smiled slowly, his eyes narrowing on her face.

'Is that a good idea?' His glance raked over her. 'Don't you think it was safer when you kept your gaze determinedly averted in terror?'

'Do you think you could stop telling me that I'm scared?' Catrina asked, fighting the urge to duck her head.

'Certainly. When you stop being scared.' The waiter came with drinks, and Zade sat back, looking at her with interest. 'Tell me about your father.'

That was easy and she began to relax. It was a safe subject. She could talk about her father for a long time, and she did.

'So how did you come to have an Italian mother?' he asked when she finally ran out of steam.

'Sheer chance. My father is doing the Far East runs at the moment, but he used to cover Europe. My mother was a stewardess with the Italian airline and she was in London on leave. When she flew home it just happened to be my father's plane. One of the stewardesses was suddenly ill on the way and my mother explained who she was, took off her jacket, and helped. When they landed in Rome my father came back to thank her, took her for a drink, and that was it.'

'Love at first sight?'

'Yes. A quite astonishing love. You could tell it was there. It used to be almost visible, floating in the air.'

She suddenly stopped, embarrassed, and he was watching her expression closely.

'But you don't feel like that about Gary.'

It was a flat statement, no question, and Catrina felt tricked and angry. He didn't really want to take her to lunch. He was still summing her up.

'Is this the reason for the lunch, Mr Mackensie? You want to know if I'll do for Gary? You're still checking me out?'

'Checking you out? What the hell has it got to do with me?' he bit out, instantly angry himself. 'I'm just trying to get to know you. Stop being so prickly, Catrina, and call me Zade. I'm not yet ninety.'

'I'm sorry. I can't seem to stop——'

'Defending yourself? I'm not attacking. If I was, you'd know. It's still too hot in here,' he muttered irritably, getting on with his meal.

'Is it very cold where you live?' Catrina asked, eager to change the subject from herself, because he didn't look scathing any more—he looked very annoyed indeed.

'Too scared to ask where?' he rasped. 'I live in Montana, and, yes, it's cold in winter, especially in the mountains.'

'You mean the Rockies?' He just nodded, hardly glancing at her, evidently too cross to speak, and she rushed on, 'Don't you have the house heated—the ranch house?'

'Naturally.' He looked at her tauntingly. 'I don't live in a wooden shack I built myself. You're quite the little innocent, aren't you, Catrina? Is it youth, upbringing, or a natural trait?'

'A desire to pretend ignorance and boost up your soaring ego,' Catrina snapped, meeting his derisive glance with flashing dark eyes. It brought one of those devastating smiles and he raised his glass to her.

'Well done. It's a good job I came after all. Before I go I'll have you trained to beat down Gary's mother in a shouting match.'

'I don't need...!' She started out crossly, glaring at him, but he went on grinning and she gave in, laughing and flushed, tingling all over.

'Peace, Catrina,' he suggested softly, his eyes narrowed on her flushed face. 'I can see the Italian in you.'

She could feel it herself and it astonished her. She couldn't remember ever being fiery before in her life.

'Why come to England for the sort of reception you're undoubtedly getting?' she asked with a quick glance at him, very anxious to change the subject and have those blue eyes less assessing.

'Apart from my mother, Gary's my only blood-relative. Of course, there's my aunt, but she's definitely not counted. I suppose too that I like to come back to my roots from time to time.' He glanced sourly out of the window at the grey sky. 'I think this will be the last time, though. I could be lying on a beach in the West Indies.'

'Do you get away much?' Catrina asked, fascinated by his lean, handsome face.

'About every two years. Bart's health is dodgy and if I left things with the foreman Bart would just be up and doing. I haven't been back here for a while, though. This is different.' He looked up and caught her wide-eyed gaze and their eyes locked together for a minute. Catrina frantically tore her gaze back to her food.

She didn't talk after that and neither did Zade. He was finishing his lunch and probably eager to go now, but Catrina was carefully avoiding his eyes, because she had suddenly recognised the feeling that came every time their eyes met. It was excitement, excitement like an electrical charge. It was also the source of her fear and temper. She thought frantically about Gary, but Zade's face was the only thing that would come into her mind, even though she carefully avoided looking at him.

Later, in the foyer, she made an almost mad dash to get her own jacket, shrugging into it before he could help. She had to let him help with the coat, though, and having him behind her, holding it while she put it on, almost made her feel faint. Her skin was prickling and she knew her face had suddenly gone pale. He glanced at her curiously, but said nothing at all, and she was glad when they stepped outside.

His car was parked just into the parking area, close to the road, and as she stepped out towards it, Catrina felt her feet sliding from under her. She would have fallen, but Zade was too quick. His arm lashed round her and he held her firmly.

'Ice,' he muttered. 'I noticed that little patch as we came in, but I'd forgotten. Sorry.'

'It—it's hardly your fault.' His arm was still around her waist and she wanted to run, to shrug it away. Her colour was coming and going and she could hardly speak.

'It would have been my fault if you'd broken your arm,' he grunted, irritated with himself—at least, she thought he was. It might have been with her and she wouldn't have blamed him. She was behaving strangely and she knew it.

At his car she couldn't face it any longer—couldn't face sitting with him and being close, couldn't face picking up the scent of his skin, couldn't face seeing his hands on the wheel. It was all far too dangerous.

'I'll walk. Thank you so much for lunch,' she said tersely. She turned away while he was still stunned, but she didn't get far at all. His hand clamped round her wrist and he jerked her back to face him.

'What's with you? You know damned well I'm taking you back to work. It's a long walk to the library and it's bitterly cold!'

'I prefer to walk.' She tried to pull her hand away, but stopped when she saw Mrs Swift, one of the matrons of the town, slow down from her brisk pace and look at them with interest. Zade followed her gaze, his hand still tight and determined on her wrist.

'If you want a scene, Catrina, I'll make a big one for you in no time at all,' he said in a taut voice. 'Get in the car.'

With little alternative, she did, and when he was sitting beside her he turned on her angrily.

'All right, Miss Arnold,' he rasped. 'What did I do to bring this on?'

'Nothing. I just—just wanted to walk.'

'Walk? Did you?' His lean hand tilted her flushed face. 'You looked as if you wanted to run. I think maybe we're getting down to the source of your terrifying problem. You have a great desire to fight me. You're anxious when you're close to me and you're trying your damnedest to keep away. If you've got any sense, you'll not ask yourself why.'

He just started the car and drove off, too fast, and she was back outside the library within minutes. He didn't get out. In fact he didn't even look at her and Catrina dared not look at him. She was glad when the library door closed firmly behind her. He had driven off by then and she was shaken as she never had been in her life. She could still see his face, his blue eyes probing and then angry. Her wrist was red where he had gripped it and she didn't delve any deeper into her feelings.

Mrs Swift was her first customer. Her brisk pace had been in this direction and Catrina smiled at her wanly. This woman was a bosom pal of Gary's mother and an ardent gossip.

'Cold spell,' she observed as she came to bring in her book. 'Last of the winter, I expect.'

'Let's hope so,' Catrina managed cheerfully, waiting for the questions.

'My, that was a striking man you were with. Hope Gary knows.' It was heavy, forced joking, just like her smile. 'I thought for a minute he was trying to pull you into his car.'

'Oh, my goodness, no.' Catrina laughed. 'It was Gary's cousin. He used to live around here. Surely you know him?'

'Not that I remember.' It stopped her questions, but Catrina could see she was not at all satisfied. Mrs Hudson would be the next to know and then there would be more questions. Nothing happened in this little market town without the whole population being involved. Even her own wedding was a source of communal excitement, as if they owned her. She forced it all out of her mind, working furiously, doing small tasks she had put off for ages, and at four the garage delivered her car, right on time. She felt a wave of warmth. Gary had rung them and sparked them into life. He never let her down. Last night was his first transgression, and his clash with Zade had probably brought that on.

He rang when she got home, just checking that everything was all right, and she chatted quite happily until he invited her to supper.

'Oh, I can't come tonight, Gary,' she said quickly.

'Come on, Trina,' he coaxed. 'Zade will be here. I want him here every night while I can. He'll be going soon. You don't have to drive. He'll collect you and bring you back as he's staying in town.'

'No, I can't.' Even if she had been tempted his last words were enough to stop her. 'You can have a nice little talk with him. I'll just be in the way.'

'You're never in the way, love. I want you here all the time. Listen, I'll lock my mother in her room. It would please Zade anyway. You'll have noticed she doesn't take to him.'

Who did she take to? Catrina asked herself, but she gave the necessary laugh and remained adamant.

'To be quite honest, Gary, I don't feel too well. I may have a cold coming on. You just have a nice evening and you can tell me about it later.' She wouldn't be swayed so he had to accept it, and Catrina sat looking at the phone when he finally rang off. It was the first time she had ever lied to him. Now she had even more on her conscience. And why hadn't she told him that she had had lunch with his cousin?

She knew why. It was something secret inside her, something she couldn't even look at herself. It was shaming excitement, a frightening weakness, and she didn't understand it, but it would have to be controlled just for this little while until Zade left for home and safety came back to her life.

She had a bath before tea, built up the fire, and settled in front of it with her food on a tray. After that meal at lunchtime she didn't want very much and, in any case, food was a bit difficult to get down. Guilt was a choking feeling. She told herself not to be foolish, that she had done nothing wrong, but she knew inside that she had. She had felt the excitement for someone else that she should have been feeling for Gary. Her calm assessment of marriage was no longer calm at all.

The bell rang as she was taking her tray to the kitchen and she put it down to answer. To her dismay, Zade stood at the door, looking no more pleased than he had done when he had driven off after lunch. Her appearance clearly surprised him. He stared at her, his eyes running over her from her black curls to her feet.

'Going to the farm looking like that? Am I supposed to wait while you change or do you plan to give your intended a thrill and stun his mother?'

He had stopped looking furious, but there was a taut look about him that brought all Catrina's anxiety back, and the need to defend herself was uppermost.

'I'm not going.' Catrina said it as calmly as possible and he just walked in, closing the door behind him with a snap.

'Since when?' He stared down at her and she forced herself to face him with a cold look.

'Since Gary rang and asked me and I refused. He was intending to ring you and tell you, I think.'

'Well, he didn't. Anyway, I was out.' He glanced at the tray balanced precariously on the hall table. 'Been nibbling on your diet?' he enquired derisively, and Catrina came to angry life.

'I've just had a meal, if that's what you mean, and now I'm going to watch television before bed.'

'You'd rather watch television than watch Gary?' he taunted.

'Yes, I would! I'll have plenty of time to watch him when you've gone back to America.'

It was suddenly silent, a pool of emptiness into which she had thrown hard words, and his eyes had that assessing look again.

'Not very popular, am I?' he asked quietly. 'You must be in league with my aunt. Maybe I should be in the West Indies after all.'

It made her feel very ashamed and she reminded herself that he had been nothing but kind, in spite of his powerful ways. It was her, the effect he had on her.

'I'm sorry. I didn't mean to be so spiteful. I'm just a bit jumpy for some reason. You've been very kind to me and I can see why Gary likes you so much.'

'Can you, Catrina?' His hand came out and tilted her downcast face and as he touched her sparks seemed to fly from his fingertips, racing across her skin like fire, and she gasped, her face going pale. 'Lying is quite a good idea,' he said quietly. 'Just go on lying until I go. From now on, the kindness will have to be a little sparse. You take it to heart too much.'

'I—I don't know what you mean.'

'Don't you?' He let his hand slide downwards, down her neck and into the opening of her dressing-gown. It went no further, his fingers just resting lightly against her smooth shoulder, but it was enough to bring a soft cry of anxiety, enough to bring a wave of awareness that came from deep inside. She stared into his narrowed eyes and didn't understand what she saw.

'It's a good job you're not going tonight. Sooner or later Gary will notice how you act with me. What is it? You're keen on cowboys?'

'I don't——!'

'Then why didn't you slap my face, push my hand away? If you're looking for excitement, Catrina, don't look at me.'

'I'm not looking for excitement!' She knew exactly what she should have done without his telling her. She would have done it with anyone else. It was just that when he had touched her she had felt a flare of heat that had both scared and enraptured her. Now she was shaking, not with excitement, but with shame.

'No. Gary says you don't look for excitement,' he derided cruelly. 'Apparently you like to keep it at arm's length or further. Have you fixed on me with bewildered fascination or are you just growing up?'

He walked out, slamming the door, and Catrina stared after him, white-faced, shame making her cringe. Not only had she behaved so badly that he thought she was wanting him to touch her, but Gary had discussed her with Zade as if she were a peculiar specimen.

It made her feel cheap and she was glad she was alone tonight, glad that her father wasn't here. It was impossible to find relief in rage either. Zade was right. She *did* want him to touch her. It was a feeling she had never had before and it had hit her as soon as she had seen him, hit her with fright, shyness and trembling limbs. How soon would he go? Surely now he would just drive off and never come back? He had been filled with contempt and she knew she could never look him in the face again.

He thought she was chasing him when she was engaged to Gary. Gary was his cousin and Zade cared enough about him to come here to the farm and put up with his aunt's annoyance. She could understand his contempt, but she had not meant it to happen. It had just come so unexpectedly and devastated her.

There were more icy patches next morning and Catrina knew she would have to be very careful driving to work. It would probably be like this until the rain started. The high ground of the dale was always the last to feel spring. It was possible to be in very good weather lower down and then drive to an actual snow-line quite late on in the year. A little higher up the dale trees became few and far between and winter there was bitter and unrelenting.

It did not improve during the day. A watery sun tried hard, but failed to lift the mist that hung around, and by five o'clock, when the library shut, it was dark, more misty still and freezing hard. On the hills above town, when the lights had been left behind, Catrina slowed almost to a crawl, but she could feel the car trying to slide at every corner. When she at last came to the long road that had the cottage at the end she relaxed and breathed a sigh of relief.

It was a little too soon. As she pulled in by the gate, the car seemed to dance sideways, the steering useless, and there was a quite sickening thud as the front end slid towards the ditch and nosedived. It was no more than a foot, but the front wheel went straight down and

Catrina lurched forward, banging her head and seeing stars. It was a bit tricky getting out and she slipped on the road as soon as her feet touched it. At this rate she would be injured before she got into the cottage.

She collected her bag, removed her keys, and managed the path with the aid of first the railing and later the edge of the lawn. It was ridiculous, more like January than late March. By the time she was inside the cottage, the door shut behind her, she was quite exhausted and not a little shaken up.

As bumps on the head went it was negligible, but the shock was there and her leg hurt where she had fallen. It was the garage for the old monster too. Tomorrow she would need a taxi, because the local garage never opened its doors until ten. If she didn't ring them now she would be waiting even longer, because they vanished at six sharp.

She knew the owner and had to endure a few minutes of raucous teasing.

'Now what have you been doing, Catrina?' he asked loudly. 'You only got the car back yesterday.'

When she told him about the ice and the present whereabouts of her car he was a little more sympathetic.

'Front wheel right in?' he asked. 'We'll need the truck, then. How did you manage to get out? Bit of a struggle, was it?'

She told him with diminishing patience, not mentioning her fall in case he started all over again, but to her surprise he was quite caring.

'Not too badly hurt, are you, Catrina?' he asked with unexpected kindness. 'Are you having the doctor?'

Catrina told him very emphatically that she was not doing any such thing and then a customer claimed his attention and he left her with a solemn promise to get out there first thing. That meant eleven in the morning, Catrina surmised as she thankfully got rid of him.

She felt as if she had been in a minor war. Everything was aching, especially her head, and she almost staggered as she made her way to the kitchen and a welcome cup of tea. The kettle hadn't even boiled before the bell rang and she hobbled back into the hall. So far she hadn't managed to get her coat off, and at this rate she would be waiting for her cup of tea for ages.

She did think it might be the garage showing an unexpected burst of charity, but when she opened the door it was Zade. She wanted to shut it again and she even tried, but his foot put a stop to that and he looked down at her from the darkness.

'Let me in, Catrina!'

She still tried to close the door, but he put his hand out and held it open, looking down at her with concern.

'Stop it, Catrina! Are you all right?'

'Of course I'm all right,' she managed bleakly, not looking at him. 'I can't think why you're——'

'I told you to stop!' He came in and closed the door to the icy air. 'I was at the garage when your call came in. I can't imagine there are any other Catrinas in the place and I heard his end of the conversation. I came straight up. I thought you might need help.'

'I—I don't. Why didn't you call Gary?' she asked desperately.

'I was closest.' He stared at her hard, his eyes locked with hers. 'Why didn't you?' It was another challenge, another accusation, and she glared up at him, pushing away the frightening weakness that had come over her the moment she had seen him. Fighting her way out of this was the only sensible thing to do.

'Because I haven't had time. First the garage, then you. I haven't even taken my coat off yet. I haven't had a drink of tea!' She went on glaring, too upset to be aware of the excitement of his presence, and he reached out to her face.

'Let me look at that bump.'

'Don't touch me!' She sprang back, almost falling, but he caught her, muttering under his breath in annoyance. He lifted her and carried her into the lighter kitchen, sitting her on the table and standing over her angrily.

'You are something else!' he snapped. 'Somebody has to see to you and I'm here. Stop acting as if I'm a well-known pervert!' She looked at him wildly, ridiculously shaken, and he shook his head in exasperation. 'Now just try to be sensible and sit still while I find out what you've done to yourself.'

He was obviously determined to help even if it killed him, and she sat very still, tight and hard, not looking at him now, her eyes closed as he lifted her black curls and examined the bruise that was beginning to colour.

He left her and went to get water, taking the hot water she had boiled for tea, asking where the first-aid kit was and then coming back with a clean cloth.

'Just hold still and I'll bathe it,' he murmured, looking at her injury with hard, clinical eyes. It hurt more to have him touch her than to have the bruise attended to and she winced, her skin heating as his hand held her face. He said nothing. He didn't even look at her and when he stood back with satisfaction she almost sighed with relief. Now he would go. Now it was over. She felt much, much worse than she had done when the car hit the ditch, and it was Zade, not injury.

'Let's see that leg,' he ordered, and this time she refused point-blank, her face flushed but utterly determined.

'It's all right. It's just a bang. I can do it myself.'

'You're wearing woolly tights and it's torn them,' he said testily. 'So that was some bang.'

'I'll see to it! Leave me alone!' She almost shouted at him in agitation and he looked down at her seriously.

'Look, I know how it is. You want me to ring Gary and get him to come and see to you?' Catrina hung her head, shaking it, gasping with pain as it hurt.

'No.'

'Then let me do it, because I'm not leaving here until I know you're all right.'

'I don't want you to——'

'I assure you, I won't! The thought is merely in your head. Too many library books.' He slid her from the table and took her coat, looking down at her as if she were an idiot. 'You've got as long as it takes me to put this in the hall cupboard to get those tights off,' he announced forcefully.

He walked out and Catrina knew he meant it. She struggled with the tights and it made her feel awful, but she had the wild feeling that if she didn't do it, he would. The bump on her head, the bang on her leg and then Zade had left her almost dazed. She was shivering for a lot of reasons, and she was standing by the table, hanging on to sanity by a thin thread, when he walked back in. He just lifted her back to the table without a word and when he touched her leg she drew back, trying to get away from him.

'Oh, please, Zade,' she cried out pitifully, but he didn't even look up.

'Grit your teeth,' he muttered. 'With a bit of luck we'll both get out of this alive.'

She kept her eyes closed as he bathed her leg, steeling herself not to tremble, asking herself why he had come to do this when he could have just ignored it all. He could just have asked if she was all right and then gone. She hadn't wanted him here. She had tried to shut him out. He had his hand beneath her knee and she was frightened. Her leg was stinging, but it didn't seem to matter. His fingers on her skin were burning and she wanted him to go on touching her. She was ashamed of the feelings she had never had before.

'I tried to make you go!' she suddenly burst out angrily. 'I tried to shut the door. Why are you doing this? Why have you come? I can manage by myself. I always manage by myself. I don't want you here. What are you going to say next, that I did it deliberately to get you here? I don't want you here! I don't want you anywhere near me!'

'I know.' He suddenly lifted her down and walked through into the sitting-room with her, putting her on the settee and turning to stir up the fire she had left banked down that morning. Then he walked out and Catrina kept her eyes shut, hoping he would go, knowing that once again she had made a fool of herself.

He walked back in with a cup of tea and put it on the coffee-table.

'It's sweet, whether you like it or not. You're shocked.' She looked up at him then with brown eyes filled with bright tears and started to giggle. Shocked? She was almost destroyed! She dreaded his hand touching hers, but he had held her face, gently wiped her head, touched her leg. She was more than shocked; she felt as if she were on another planet with no air.

Catrina couldn't stop laughing and then she couldn't stop crying and he pulled her forward, holding her tightly.

'Stop it, Catrina. Try to calm down. It's all right. I understand.' His deep voice did the trick and soon she was just making soft little sounds that were the end of self-inflicted misery.

When he handed her a white handkerchief she wiped her face and muttered almost inaudibly, 'I'm sorry. I didn't mean to do that.'

'Forget it. In any case, I imagine it's my fault. I should have left you or called Gary.'

'Why didn't you?' She looked up at him with huge, dark eyes and his face hardened.

'Stupidity!' he snapped. 'Don't start again! I can do without your soft-eyed looks of bewitchment!'

The retaliation was so swift, so hard that she gave a little cry of pain and turned her face away. Zade swore softly under his breath and turned her face back, staring into her eyes and then searching angrily for her mouth.

'All right, Catrina,' he rasped against her lips. 'Let's see what it's like, shall we? Tell me if you think you've found what you're looking for after this.'

'This,' was a deep and searching kiss that was almost a punishment, his arms tightly around her, crushing her against his hard body. He probed until she opened her mouth and then his tongue slid inside roughly, searching for hers and refusing to stop the almost violent caressing.

It was an intimacy that shook her world and turned it over. His hand behind her head was like steel, giving her no escape, his probing tongue sending piercing feelings down into her legs. All coherent thought left her and she just submitted like a slave.

He let her go when she couldn't stop shaking and he stood with one lithe and angry movement, turning to the fireplace and looking into the growing flames.

'Stick to Gary,' he grated. 'He knows how to handle you. Grown-ups have other demands to make, not just nice, tidy kisses.'

Somehow she got herself up, making for the door before he knew, her lips bruised with a savage kiss that had been an insolent chastisement. Zade had punished her cruelly for her temerity and she was trembling from head to foot, but she managed to speak with dignity.

'Please let yourself out and see that the door latches.'

As she opened the sitting-room door his hand hit it, forcing it closed again, and she looked up in shock.

Zade's face was tight, frustrated and pale beneath the tan.

'Catrina! I'm sorry. I did that, not you. You tried to shut me out, tried to make me go. I should have called Gary, and don't ask me again why I didn't.'

CHAPTER FOUR

CATRINA didn't ask, but her wide eyes asked, her trembling mouth asked without words, and Zade looked down at her, his eyes never leaving her softly bruised lips.

'All right,' he said quietly. 'I wanted to come myself. I wanted to see you and make sure you were all right. I had to know.' His brilliant eyes moved over her face. 'I wanted to see you looking at me like that,' he added softly.

Catrina looked away quickly, her face flushing with nervous excitement, and he groaned, pushing her back against the door, holding her face up with one strong hand. 'Do you think I don't feel it too? I should have left town the moment I saw you. I've been hanging around like a villain, waiting to get my hands on you.'

'You—you'll have to go,' she whispered, darts of flame starting deep inside and rising to hit her all over. 'You don't mean it. Even if you did——'

'Even if I did you're going to be my cousin's wife,' he agreed thickly. He looked down at her and then drew her into his arms as if he hated it. His lips came back to hers, but this time not bruising, this time searching and probing, moving over her mouth with an urgency that stopped her heart for a minute.

It came then—the excitement, the heat, the feelings she had never possessed, and she swayed forward, soft and eager, moaning against his mouth, opening her lips when he demanded it.

'Again, Catrina,' he ordered unevenly. 'Open your mouth for me.'

He spun her round, leaning against the door, holding her to him, devouring her with hard, warm lips, and she could hear her own voice whimpering, feel the hard power of his body against hers.

'You've come to life,' he muttered thickly. 'I've been hungry for this since I first saw you.'

His hands ran over her as she clung to his neck and he pulled her even closer, holding her against his demanding body and sliding his hand beneath her thin sweater, finding her skin and then moving ruthlessly to her breast with no waiting.

It was the first time. So many first times. She had never felt on fire before, never been close to fainting with delight, never felt a man's hands on her skin. He knew it and he lifted his head, his burning blue gaze holding hers as his fingers teased her breast, sending shafts of pleasure through her. He just kept on looking at her, his eyes like fire.

'You like this, Catrina?' he asked huskily.

'Please, Zade!' She called out frantically and he covered her mouth with hungry lips, his hand cupping the swollen silk of her breast, his fingers circling the tight, pained nipple until she just fell against him, quite beyond any resistance, only seeking pleasure and desire. His body had hardened and she melted into it without a thought.

When he lifted her away from him she could scarcely open her eyes. Her body still yearned towards him and he moved away, looking down at her with bitter, frustrated eyes.

'My God! I'm stark, raving mad!'

He pulled the door open and strode into the hall, and she heard the front door open too and then bang shut. She couldn't walk, couldn't think. She just collapsed slowly to the floor, sitting there with her eyes closed, her heart racing, her body trembling and not her own any more.

As the magic eased she got slowly to her feet, making her way shakily to the bedroom. She didn't understand Zade at all but she understood herself. If Zade signalled her she would just go to him. Her whole world had crumbled because she knew she could not be Gary's wife. She would be cheating him and cheating herself. It was Zade she wanted.

Suddenly there was no future. She was going to hurt Gary and when she did she would be hurting herself. She had been swept into the danger of brilliant blue eyes and she couldn't get out. When would her father get back? She couldn't remember. His visits were never certain in any case. Nothing would wait. It was up to her to act and nobody could help her.

The next day her head was still throbbing, but she went to work by taxi, ordering it to collect her at five. She had to explain over and over to the people who came in to get books, everyone enquiring about her bruised head. Each time she explained she was back in Zade's arms, feeling his hands on her, feeling it so strongly that she imagined they all knew.

Gary walked in at five, smiling and filled with concern.

'I've cancelled your taxi,' he said as she looked up in surprise. 'Zade phoned this morning and said you'd had an accident with the car. He said you weren't hurt much. I would have come straight away, but Mother took the call. I was out. She only just told me.'

Catrina wondered what Zade had said. Had he told Gary that he had been to the cottage last night? She wanted to keep Zade out of this, not for his sake, but for Gary's. Gary thought the world of his cousin. She was not breaking that up. It was a good job he was here. What she had to say was not for his mother's ears.

On the way home it started to rain and Gary grunted in satisfaction.

'At last! End of the cold spell. It's about time. It's the first of April.' It was too late for Catrina, though. If there had been no ice she wouldn't have had an accident, Zade would not have come, and she would not have known what it was like to feel the power, the bliss of hard masculine demands. She would not have known that she needed desire. She would not have hurt Gary. The first of April, April Fool's Day! Was that what she was, a fool?

When they got to the cottage she asked him in, feeling utterly weary at what she had to do.

'I'll just see you're all right,' he agreed. 'I can't stop, though, Trina. I've still got some feeding to do.'

'It's important, Gary,' Catrina said quietly, leading him to the sitting-room. 'Will—will you sit down?'

'OK, love.' He looked at her with amusement, not taking it seriously. 'What's the problem?'

She couldn't think how to tell him. How did you wreck somebody's life gently? He was smiling at her and she looked back in despair. Could she tell him, could she hurt both of them? Maybe they could have a life of happiness, caring for each other as they did? Her father's words came back clearly, starkly. 'There are many kinds of love.' He had spoken of magic. Could she cheat Gary out of magic? He would never have it with her and she knew that now.

'I can't marry you, Gary.' There was, after all, only one way to say it.

He just stared at her. He didn't believe it and he reached across for her hand.

'Now, then, Trina,' he said quietly. 'You've had a shock of some sort. Things are getting you down a bit and I know Mother is all manner of a nuisance, but——'

'It's not that, Gary. If I married you I'd be ruining your life. I could never give you the sort of physical warmth you need and——'

'Look, I know that,' he interrupted firmly. 'I know you're a bit cold. It doesn't matter. When we're married you'll feel differently. After the first few times...'

It made her blood run icy-cold because for the first time she was looking things right in the face, hearing what Gary had obviously worked out for himself. She had known him for a long time, but she had never thought deeply about that even when they had planned to marry. He was her best friend. It was affection she felt for Gary, not a strong enough feeling for marriage. Losing her mother had made her very susceptible and Gary had been there all the time, determined to marry her, rushing her along, not giving her time to think, and she had let him.

'I can't,' she said seriously. 'I'm sorry, Gary, but I don't love you like that. You're close to me, dear to me, my dearest friend, but it's not enough.'

'How many times have you said you love me?' he persisted.

'A lot of times, and I do, but——'

'You can get help for this frigidity problem,' he told her briskly. 'You can see somebody. We'll go together. I want you and you'll want me soon enough.'

Catrina just stared at him wonderingly. At one time she would have believed it. She would have believed that she needed help. Now she knew it was not true. She had feelings when Zade held her, kissed her, even when he simply looked at her.

'I can't marry you, Gary. How I feel about you is not going to change and I'm not ruining your life.'

She took off her ring and handed it to him and he stood and looked down at her with a grim expression growing on his face.

'You're having a damned good try,' he pointed out bleakly. 'I'm going to leave you for now, Trina. It's just something that's come over you—maybe it's wedding nerves. I'll tell Mother we're putting it off till August after all. That will give you time to calm a bit. You'll be getting this ring back soon enough, though.'

It was no use. He brushed aside everything she said and Catrina became more and more agitated. She felt backed into a corner, faced with fighting her way out, and she realised that this was not an entirely new feeling with Gary.

'I'm not marrying you, Gary,' she insisted and there must have been something about her face that convinced him because his own face hardened.

'There's somebody else,' he said coldly, watching her like a hunter.

'There's nobody else. How could there be? I just know it wouldn't work and I don't want you wasting your life.'

'Because you love me, your dearest friend?' he snapped. 'Time will tell.' He walked from the room, letting himself out, and Catrina sat staring into space. She had taken a step that was irreversible. There was nothing to take its place, just this mad, bewildering craving for a man who despised himself for kissing her.

Her father rang later, but he wasn't coming home— the turn-around time was too short—and Catrina kept her voice deliberately cheerful. It did not work at all. Her father knew her too well.

'Enough of the weather, Cat,' he ordered. 'Tell me what's wrong.'

She was going to say that nothing was wrong—after all, nobody could help. He would have to know some time, though, and she didn't want to lie.

'I'm not getting married,' she said quietly, trying to sound calm. 'It wouldn't work out.'

'Have you had a row, love?' he asked sympatheti-
cally, and at least she was able to say no with conviction.
How Gary would behave later was a little worrying, but
for now he had taken it calmly enough.

'No. He took it well. I told him this evening.'

'It's your life, Cat, but why?'

'I—I don't love him like that. We would never have
been happy, not just me, but Gary too. I was all mixed
up, Dad. I'm very fond of Gary and it seemed to be
enough. I hadn't realised that——'

'But now you do? Who is it, love?'

'Nobody! You don't understand.'

'Perhaps I do. Perhaps I'm very glad. Remember what
I told you, Cat? There are many kinds of love, but one
kind is magic.'

When he rang off she went to bed, his words ringing
round in her head. There were many kinds of magic,
too. She wasn't going to confuse desire with love. She
had never felt the thrill before and maybe she would
never feel it again. Perhaps Zade was right and she was
only just growing up? Whatever it was, she expected
Zade to go now, back to his own country. He would
never know, even in the unlikely event that she met him
again.

The chances were slim indeed because she wouldn't
be going to Gary's farm any more and she knew that
Zade was only here for a short time. In an odd sort of
way, it was none of his business, and Catrina was quite
sure he would think that too. If he thought anything else
it would be that she was letting his beloved cousin down.

He thought it. Her car would take a couple of days
and as the taxi dropped her off at home the next evening
she walked up the path to find Zade waiting at the door
in the shadows of the porch.

'What do you want?' She was instantly alert, gripping
her house key tightly, standing well clear of him. It was

still murky weather, even though the sharp cold had gone, and she was glad of the gloom. If anyone saw Zade here there would be gossip all over town. So far Gary had not been in touch and he certainly knew nothing about Zade's visits. If he found out the hurt would go much deeper and she could not allow that.

'I want to take a close look at insanity,' Zade rasped. 'I had Gary on the phone.'

'What Gary and I do is none of your business,' she managed icily. 'Our problems are private.'

'Not if I've caused them.' He reached forward and took her key, jabbing it in the lock and turning it. 'Inside! I'm not conducting a conversation on the doorstep.'

'There's no conversation necessary,' Catrina informed him tersely. 'Just go.'

'The hell I will!' As she flicked on the hall lights he stepped in behind her, closing the door, and one glance at his tall, angry frame warned her that she was incapable of putting him out again.

Her only defence was indifference and she walked away as calmly as possible, taking off her coat and going into the sitting-room to stir the fire into life. He followed and stood, tall and intimidating, in the doorway, leaning against the frame and following her progress with cold blue brilliance, eyes that seemed to shoot flames at her.

'What's all this about not getting married?' he rasped. 'Do you know what you've done to Gary?'

'What *I've* done?' She turned on him with flashing dark eyes, her short black curls tossing wildly. 'I've saved him from a future of misery, that's what I've done, and it hurt me to do it.'

'Don't be so stupid!' he bit out. 'Do you imagine you're the only girl in the world to have been kissed by somebody other than the man she's going to marry? Do you have to let it go madly to your head and ruin your life?'

'What an ego you have,' Catrina seethed, glaring at him. 'That—that episode has nothing to do with this. I love Gary too much to make his future a misery.'

'You *love* him?' Zade looked at her as if she were wickedly deranged. His eyes were narrowed in anger, his face tight. 'You've sure got a funny way of proving it!'

'I am proving it,' Catrina said more quietly. 'Gary needs more than I can give. A man doesn't want a wife who——'

'Who's sexually cold?' Zade looked at her derisively. 'He told me about your problem.' His gaze ran over her, lingering from head to foot. 'I didn't correct him.'

Catrina blushed painfully, but she held her ground, managing to meet the scathing blue eyes.

'As you're so close to Gary—close enough to hear our private affairs—perhaps he told you his solution? I can seek help. But, better still, his first choice is that I can get used to it the hard way, over a period of time.'

Zade didn't say anything at all. He just looked at her quite starkly. His lips were one tight line and she couldn't make up her mind whether she saw temper or shock on his face. She certainly did not see derision. It gave her a very unhappy satisfaction. She had managed to shut him up, to still that biting tongue, and he couldn't come up with a smart, stinging answer to her words at all.

'Now that you've made your official intrusion you can go,' she told him proudly, her head held high. 'I don't imagine I've heard the end of all this, but just understand that it's none of your business.'

'I caused it.' His eyes were still intently on her now pale face and she shook her head, turning away.

'No. Clear your conscience. You did Gary a favour. Some people would settle for very little, but I love Gary too much to let him do that.'

'Why do you keep saying you love him?' he bit out harshly.

'Because I do.' She turned back to him fiercely. 'I may not be as worldly as you, Mr Mackensie, but I can tell the difference between love and desire. One is gentle, tender and sweet. The other is chemistry. Animals have that, I imagine.'

She knew she was lashing out at him as hard as possible and his eyes narrowed to icy slits, although his face didn't change at all.

'Then you've really learned something. I wonder what you're going to do with this wisdom?'

'Nothing that will drift to your ears when you're back where you came from. Now I'd like you to go, Mr Mackensie.'

A cool smile twisted his mouth as he turned.

'You did that all wrong, sugar,' he sneered. 'You can't still call me Mr Mackensie when I've kissed you senseless and caressed your breast. It just doesn't ring true.' His eyes flared over her as he turned and went into the hall.

Catrina followed, desperate to see him go and get the door locked behind him. His final words had set her pulses racing again and she wanted to be by herself and safe.

With the door open, he suddenly spun back, grasping her chin, forcing her face up to meet his eyes.

'When is your father back?'

'I—I'm not sure. In any case, he rang and I told him.'

'I don't doubt it,' he rasped. 'I'm sure he sympathised, but sympathy is not what you're going to need. I may live a long way off, but I know this town, these people. You're an outsider no matter how long you've been here. You've hurt one of their own and my aunt will make sure they know, even though she's probably laughing up her sleeve. What you're going to need, *Miss Arnold*, is protection, because they'll hurt you back in any way they can.'

He went and she almost fell on the door to lock it. She was more upset than she had been when she had had to tell Gary, and it wasn't just Zade's last words. She felt as if she had been in a very bitter battle, hurt and hurting.

She had no idea if she had done the right thing at all. Gary had not been too angry, but she knew deep down that when he realised her determination he would be very angry. She had seen him angry before with his mother, though never with her. He would be back as soon as he had let it all sink in. Like Zade, she thought of her father, and wished him here most desperately. The house seemed big, empty and lonely, almost worrying.

Catrina shook her head and pulled herself up smartly. What was she doing, frightening herself? It was Zade, the way he made her feel, the courage it had taken to meet his blazing eyes. Gary was kind, gentle. He would come back, of course, but it would be to talk things over quietly, and she needed that too.

Next day Catrina looked out of the window to see a sky that had miraculously cleared of both rain and mist. The cold wind still blew across the dale, but the deadly, heavy sky was now high and blue. She could almost feel spring in the air and it lightened her spirits a little. Today she only had to work until lunchtime. It was Saturday. There would be a rush because it was market day, but by twelve-thirty she would be on her way home.

All the way to town in the taxi she felt herself tightening up. Zade's final words had really got through to her because she knew how true they were. He had lived here until he was sixteen. His parents had been born here; his cousin and aunt still lived in the dale. He might now be an American, but in many ways he was more acceptable than she was.

Her mother and father had bought the cottage several years ago, but she had already been eighteen and her father did not farm, did not have a shop, did not even stay here for any length of time. He had a job they thought glamorous and rather unnecessary. For herself, she had been accepted as Gary's girl for the past two years, and it had changed their slightly suspicious attitude.

Now she had hurt Gary, rejected him. That was how they would look at it. It would be a sort of communal shame, somebody jilted. If it had been the other way round they would have shrugged their shoulders, but it was not the other way round at all, and there was Gary's mother. She would make the most of it.

Catrina expected attack right from the first and steeled herself for it, but nothing happened and by eleven o'clock she knew that nothing was about to happen. She felt guilty, foolish. How could she have thought that Gary would go round telling everybody? In all probability he hadn't even told his mother. He had just confided in Zade because Zade had always been his hero.

It hurt that he had told Zade about them, about her coldness. Even so, she forgave Gary. Maybe he had been so worried that he had really needed to talk, and who better than his cousin? He would not know that Zade would use the information to hurt her.

When it was almost twelve, the garage man came with her car and gave her a very amusing lecture on driving. At least, he found it amusing, but Catrina only wanted to be off home. She had been on edge almost all the time and she knew what she was going to do this afternoon—she was going into the garden. It was time to do a few jobs and it would clear her head.

By one o'clock she was in her jeans and wellington boots, her anorak and a thick sweater, a bright woollen cap pulled over her short black curls. It was cold, but not so bitter in the front garden, away from the north-easterly wind. It was time to take the dead heads off the hydrangeas if she wanted a good show later, and she set about the task vigorously, her secateurs in her hand and her mind blanking out trouble.

She was working close to the house when Gary came and she just stood up and watched his car stop by the gate. She didn't know quite how to act. Should she behave as if they were still the best of friends? Should she greet him as she always did with a kiss on the cheek? He would have to make the move, and as he got out of the car she knew he would not be smiling down at her and trying to kiss her.

He walked up the path and he looked almost like another person. He looked hard and bitter and she knew he had spent that time away just brooding about it. Not that she blamed him. She had struck a devastating blow at him, not least at his masculinity, and she knew she could not really have expected him to take it lightly.

'Have you changed your mind again?' he asked when she smiled at him. 'Does that smile mean we're back together or is it a smile for a good old friend?'

'I haven't changed my mind, Gary,' she said quietly. 'If I hadn't meant it, I wouldn't have said something so terrible.'

'Oh! So you do know it was terrible?' he rasped. 'You do know it's knocked the life from me? Did you also know it's going to make me the laughing-stock of the dale?'

'Why should it? All they need know is that we changed our minds.'

'I didn't change my mind, Trina,' he informed her tightly, stepping nearer. 'I've wanted you since I first saw you at eighteen and I thought I'd got close. I've played your cool little game and I've waited. Now you've snatched it all away. I won't be changing my mind.'

'Gary.' She looked up at him patiently, prepared to take some harsh words, considering them to be only what she deserved. 'Can't we talk quietly about this?'

'All right. Let's go inside.'

Catrina looked up at him and suddenly knew she dared not. This was not Gary, not the Gary she knew. Underneath there was violence. It was written in his eyes, in the tight edge to his mouth, and even the garden seemed to be a dangerous place.

'Let's talk here,' she managed cheerfully. 'I'm enjoying the sunshine. It's ages since the sun shone at all.'

'What's wrong, Trina?' he asked grimly, stepping closer still. 'Are you scared to go into the house with me?'

'Of course not!' She gave a laugh that was not returned and he stared down at her, looking big and angry.

'Maybe you should be. An hour alone with you and I'd settle all your anxieties. I'm the help you need with your physical problems. By evening you wouldn't have any.'

She really saw violence then, something she had never seen and never suspected. Her skin went cold because she knew what he was threatening and she knew he actually meant it. He took hold of her arm, towering over her, and she was too scared to even pull away—scared and utterly disbelieving. She had been seeing him for two years, been engaged for over six months. It couldn't be Gary. He moved her slowly towards the door and she felt panic wash over her. She hadn't locked the door behind her. He only had to open it.

A car came gliding up to the gate and Gary turned his head furiously, but the angry tension drained away as Zade stepped out of the car and shouted across the garden.

'There you are! I called at the farm, but your mother said you were on your way here. Not going to the market?'

'In a minute. I called to see Trina.' There was still rage at the back of Gary's voice, but he was gradually controlling it, gradually pulling himself back to normal. Only now Catrina didn't know what was normal. At this moment she felt she knew Zade better and she was still trembling with fright, still unable to even speak.

'Gardening?' Zade asked pleasantly. He looked at her steadily and there was neither a warning nor a question in his eyes. 'Care to break for tea—you make it?'

It was so natural, so calm that Gary's suspicious stance relaxed altogether and to Catrina's amazement he grinned at her.

'Good idea. Just what I was about to suggest myself.'

When she invited them inside and sat on the step to remove her muddy boots it was Gary who bent and pulled them off, his eyes meeting hers with a smile. She wondered if he was mad. Her glance flashed to Zade, but he was just standing in the hall, watching, no expression at all on his face.

It was the most bizarre of tea-parties. Catrina couldn't manage to say anything, but Gary talked in his usual manner to Zade and Zade answered with all the amusing talent he had, but he knew. Catrina was sure he knew and when he looked across at her she bit her lip and let her eyes slide away.

'Good grief! I'll miss the market!' Gary suddenly jumped up and put his cup on to the tray. 'If I do, I'll never hear the end of it. Mother wants about a ton of things.' He glanced at Zade. 'Coming?'

'To the market? No way! I'm coming, though. I'm going back to the hotel.'

They walked to the gate together and Catrina went with them. She wasn't exactly sure how to behave.

Danger had brushed very close by and there was nobody to run to, nobody to tell. She might even have been imagining the worst of it.

Gary got into his car, but Zade just stood by his, the keys in his hand as if he was all set to go.

'Coming for dinner tonight?' Gary asked, looking up at his cousin.

'If Aunty has invited me,' Zade assured him wryly.

'Hey, I have! She's not the boss nowadays. See you at seven?'

Zade nodded and put his keys in the car door and Gary roared away. Whatever he suspected it in no way involved Zade. He had not invited Catrina. He hadn't even looked at her, and when Zade turned back to look at her as Gary's car raced out of sight her face was white as a sheet.

'All right?' He looked down at her and she nodded, nibbling away at her lip, and trying to appear normal. He could see that she was not normal and he came back inside the garden. 'What did I walk into?'

'I—I suppose you could call it an argument,' she said, telling Zade because she had nobody else to tell.

'What else could you call it?' he asked quietly, and she ducked her head to avoid his eyes.

'I don't know.' He took her arm and started up the path to the door, moving her along with him, but she still felt surrounded by danger. 'Gary might come back.'

'He won't. He won't come back because *I* came. I might just have stayed here talking and he won't risk that.'

Inside he just pushed her into the sitting-room and went off to make some more tea and she sat staring into the fire, wondering what had happened to her life. She had started out to save Gary from misery and now she felt she had saved herself from something much worse. The town, the dale, even the cottage were suddenly part of an alien landscape. Fear was at the back of her mind—not the fear she had been aware of with Zade, but the fear of her own feelings. This was real fear, cold, hard and bitter, something she had never felt before in her whole life.

Zade came back and sat down, pouring tea and handing her a cup.

'Talk!' he ordered when she just sat there silently. He reached across and pulled her cap off, dropping it on the settee, his hand ruffling her curls.

'There's nothing to say. He came and I was outside. He was angry almost at once. He said I'd made a fool of him. He—he threatened to—to...'

Zade watched her grimly and she looked up with tragic eyes.

'It's all my fault, you know, Zade.' He didn't correct her; he just went on looking at her.

'I wonder if you would still feel that guilt, if I hadn't come when I did?' he asked darkly, and she felt panic rising as her imagination took wing.

'Why did you come? I—I know I'm asking that again, but——'

'His mother said he was on his way here. I could guess how it would turn out. I know Gary. It's not only as a kid that I pulled him out of scrapes. Every time I've been here it's happened again. There's violence deep down inside him and some sort of belief that he can do exactly as he likes. Before your time, we used to go down to the city when I was here. I used to come more often then because Bart was still hale and hearty. I've knocked Gary down more than once to get him out of trouble.'

'But—but he adores you!' Catrina said in astonishment.

'He respects me.' Zade corrected. 'I'm bigger, harder and just a touch more mean, and he knows it.'

'I've known him a long time. I never even thought for a minute——'

'That he would drag you in here and put you out of your misery?' Zade bit out, and Catrina went even more pale.

'It was just temper.'

'Was it? I saw the temper on his face before I even stopped the car. I've seen it before. I saw your face too.' He stood up abruptly and paced about. 'When the devil is that father of yours due back? Does he imagine you can manage by yourself? You should be in a safe flat or something, in London, so he could be there each flight in.'

'This—this is our home! I've never felt frightened There was my mother. Until last year she was here with me and, in any case, there was Gary. I always thought there was Gary.'

'Oh, there's Gary all right!' he snapped. 'There'll be Gary for a long time to come. He won't sit down under this. If you start seeing somebody else, he'll go for them and you.'

'He wouldn't! You can't mean it!'

'I mean it! Get that firmly into your curly head. The person you finally turn to had better be built like a house.'

'I just can't believe he'll go on and on. Finally he'll calm down.'

'No, Catrina. He'll simmer. You've dented his ego, thwarted his plans, lowered his dignity. The only person you're safe with is me.' He looked at her steadily and she stared into his eyes, too shocked to feel anything but bewilderment.

'I—I don't understand you.'

'It must be that blow to your head,' he muttered making for the door. 'Lock yourself in. Keep yourself locked in and conduct your arguments by phone. Call me if he comes back at all.'

'He'll just be more angry than ever then.'

'No. He'll be scared.' He turned at the door and looked back at her. 'I scare people; haven't you fathomed that out yet?'

CHAPTER FIVE

CATRINA'S father came home that night. After his call she had not expected him—she had prepared her mind for being alone.

'I did a swap,' he said quietly. 'It's not exactly the thing to do, but as far as I'm concerned you come first.'

'I'm all right, you know.' She wasn't, but what could he do? He could not stay around to protect her and she was not even sure if she needed protection anyway. She still couldn't quite believe it all. There was no point in making her father anxious.

She told him again about her decision and this time they did not go out to eat. They sat by the fire after she had cooked a meal and she told him how she felt.

'Tell me the truth, Cat,' he said quietly. 'Is there somebody else?'

'No.' It was almost true. Zade made her feel weak, his touch set her on fire, but it was not love. It couldn't be. She hardly knew him.

'Then why have you changed your mind? Why have you suddenly looked at things differently?'

'I—I thought I could be a good wife, happy and making Gary happy, even though—even though...'

'Even though you don't want to sleep with him? Oh, Cat. You're a crazy girl. Well, thank goodness you came to your senses. You know what I'm asking, though, and you can tell me to mind my own business.'

'I realised after all that I did have potential for—that,' she managed carefully.

'I see.' He was looking at her closely and she saw a smile that he was trying hard to hide in his eyes. He thought she had fallen in love, fallen in love as he had with her mother. He didn't see at all. He didn't see that it was just chemistry, just a different sort of magic that would all go away.

She didn't disillusion him.

'How did Gary take it?' he asked, and it was dangerous ground again, but this time worse.

'He's hurt.' She looked away into the fire and he nodded.

'He would be. Poor Gary. He'll recover. You did the right thing. Well, I'm glad I came home. I expected to see you in floods of tears, very unhappy, but you're not. That alone should tell you that you did the right thing.'

She smiled and kept her thoughts to herself. Her fear was kept to herself too. Her father had to go away again and she would be on her own, because she knew she would not call Zade. He had just happened to touch the edge of her life. He had changed it, though. If she had not met him she would never have known.

Her father had to leave on Monday morning. He pulled away from the house as she set off for work and she knew he might not be back for two whole weeks. He had come home to see her and now he owed a flight to somebody else. She was on her own, completely on her own, and it clouded the day.

Catrina knew there would be trouble almost as soon as she parked her car. The people she met on her way round to the library door just nodded and never spoke; some even avoided her eyes. There was a different atmosphere and she tightened up inside at once. They knew.

To an outsider it would seem ridiculous, but Catrina knew their ways. Nothing ever happened here from one week to the next, but now something had happened.

Normally they would take sides—it would be a nine-day wonder, a source of conversation. There would be no sides taken this time because she was an outsider.

She was glad to get into the library and shut the door, but she was well aware that soon she would have to open it, and she didn't know what would happen then. Would they shun the place? Would they scorn to come even if they wanted a book? Of course there might be a few who would be sympathetic, but they would keep right out of this. They had to live here too, and memories were long in this dale.

Women came. Of course her customers were almost all women in the mornings, but this morning there wasn't even an old man coming to change a book. Nobody spoke and when she said good morning they ignored her. They didn't ignore each other, though. She had never attempted to enforce any sort of silence here because it was mostly a meeting-place and they always whispered to each other.

This morning they seemed to be meeting in little groups behind the rows of books. The ones who were looking for a book were only doing it in a desultory manner. Each time she looked up at least two of them were watching her, their lips primly disapproving. A few left, but most of them stayed, gossiping under their breath and not at all concerned if she knew.

Of course, others came, so there was a vaguely changing population of censorious women, mostly middle-aged, because the others were at work, and when Mrs Swift walked in Catrina knew with one look who had collected information from Gary's mother and who had orchestrated this show of communal condemnation.

With Mrs Swift's arrival, the atmosphere changed. The leader had arrived and outrage grew. They grew much more bold and now stood right in the middle of the floor for the most part and they were not exactly doing anything that Catrina could confront them with. The gossip was still whispered in accordance with library rules and you couldn't ask someone who glanced at you spitefully from time to time to leave. All the same, it was very upsetting, and Catrina began to seethe with annoyance. How dared they behave as if it were any of their business?

'Could I ask you to get on with choosing your books?' she said sharply.

'This is a public place,' Mrs Swift informed her with equal sharpness. 'It's called the *public* library!'

'It certainly is,' Catrina snapped, 'and a library is where people choose a book. I suggest you get on with it now. There's a tea-room across the road if you want to gossip. I'm sure they'll be glad of the custom.'

'We're not breaking any rules!'

'That depends on how you look at it,' Catrina pointed out furiously. 'I'm the librarian and I'm asking you all to choose your books and go.'

Of course they ignored her. One or two looked sheepish, but by and large she might just as well have kept quiet, and she couldn't put them all out bodily. She was almost in tears of rage when Zade walked in.

He noticed nothing immediately although he had to dodge round the ladies to get to the counter. When Catrina looked up at him, though, his eyes narrowed, and he spun round, seeing her tormentors at work.

The gossips had stopped as he opened the door and they were now looking at both of them, reassessing the situation. They did not do it for long. Zade didn't speak, but his gaze travelled over each face like a hard blue spotlight and each pair of inquisitive eyes that got the benefit of the icy blast suddenly dropped. The group split up, quite demoralised, and as they wandered back to the shelves Zade looked down at Catrina.

'How long has this been going on?' he asked in a low, hard voice.

'Since opening time.' It was now eleven and it had been a long time. 'I've pointed out the error of their ways, but they ignored me. Apart from picking them up one by one and tossing them into the street there's nothing I can do.'

'We'll see!'

Zade's hand hit the bell on the counter hard enough to make the books there jump. It had the same effect on Catrina's customers.

'The library is closing,' he announced harshly. He glanced at his watch. 'In exactly two minutes.'

'It's not time!' There was a chorus of protest and obviously they just could not believe it.

'Unusual circumstances bring about unusual events,' Zade said coldly. 'Two minutes!'

Mrs Swift was made of particularly stern stuff and she sallied forth to take action. She did not, however, direct her attack at Zade. Her angry eyes were turned on Catrina.

'You have no authority to simply close early,' she said forcefully. 'You're a public servant.'

'Miss Arnold is not closing the library, madam. *I* am closing it,' Zade said icily. 'I am closing it in two minutes.'

'You have no right!'

Zade ignored her. He looked round the room, giving everyone the benefit of his cold gaze.

'When the time is up, I shall lock the door from the outside. Anyone wishing to stay may do so—locked in!'

They came in a mad rush. Some just walked out, but one or two wanted their books and, in spite of her outrage, so did Mrs Swift.

'You've not heard the last of this,' she choked at Catrina, but Catrina did not get the chance to say anything at all. She had not had the chance since Zade walked in. He just looked at his watch and said, 'One minute!'

As the door closed behind the last astounded lady he looked grimly at Catrina.

'Get your coat.' He said nothing else and she didn't think of disobedience. She was trembling with dismay mixed with temper. Gary had told his mother and he had told her everything, probably. His mother had turned the pack on her and she felt as if she had been savaged. She put on her coat and walked to the door, locking it and putting the key in her bag as they stepped outside.

They were still there; the group had re-formed on the pavement, now with more to talk about, more outrage. Zade took her arm and walked her to his car and nobody spoke because they dared not. He was right: people were afraid of him, but at this moment Catrina wanted the hard, masculine strength. At this moment he was everything she needed.

In the car she sat in silence and Zade didn't say a word. She knew she was leaving her own car behind, but it was only a vague thought. She wanted to simply get away.

'My car...' Zade just stared grimly ahead, leaving the town fast.

'It can wait. I doubt if they'll vandalise it. They have much better methods than that.'

She knew exactly what he meant. She was too numb to think straight and the tyres of Zade's car were screaming at every corner. He was white with fury and he was getting her home fast. Her own annoyance had been a very puny thing at the side of his.

When they reached the house Zade took her key, letting them both in and locking the door firmly behind them. Catrina didn't even give a thought to that. As far as she was concerned she was temporarily safe. She wanted to lick her wounds and think things out.

She just walked straight up the stairs and Zade didn't try to stop her. He went into the sitting-room and she could hear him stirring up the fire before she had even reached her room. He would soon know the place as well as she did. Gary had never come here unless her father was here and the only time she had been alone with him in the cottage was when she had told him she would not marry him. Had there been a deep instinct for all that time to protect herself?

It was funny, but she didn't feel that with Zade. It was just safe knowing he was downstairs. What would she have done if he had not walked into the library today? Would those terrible women have finally spoken outright? And could she have stood up to an open attack? It was her job. This was her home. She would have to face them. There was tomorrow and plenty of days to come, but all the pleasure had gone out of it. She didn't belong in this town and she knew it. They would never let her forget, either.

In her heart she knew that Gary's mother had not even started yet. This had been just a preliminary attack, a shot across the bows. If she had not expected it, if Zade had not warned her, she would have been devastated. She would not have understood. It was bad enough as it was.

She was determined not to let the trembling shock get to her more. She wanted to change her clothes, though. She felt as if she had been very close to something unsavoury. When she was a bit more composed she would go down and thank Zade—if he stayed that long.

She put on a soft woollen dress—pale blue with a closely ribbed skirt—and she felt better, cleaner. She had never worn this to the library and at the moment she felt like getting out her library clothes and burning them. She brushed her short black curls into shining life and then went down. Outwardly she was composed and she knew she looked it, but inside she was almost defeated. Now that her temper had cooled she could see a very bleak future, a very lonely one.

Zade had not gone. He had made tea and the tray was standing on the coffee-table in the sitting-room. The fire was bright, with flames just beginning to lick around the red coals, and she was grateful for the cosy atmosphere, the great contrast to the last few hours.

She walked in and sat down, pouring the tea and handing a cup to Zade. He simply took it. He didn't ask if she felt all right; he didn't start to talk about the events. He just leaned back in the chair by the settee where she sat and stared grimly at the fire. Catrina realised that if there was to be any conversation she would have to start it herself because he was still fuming with that cold, hard rage she had seen before.

'Thank you,' she said. It almost came out as a whisper and for a minute she thought he hadn't heard. If anything, his face tightened even more. He didn't look at her, but he had heard.

'Have you recovered enough to make any sort of plan?'

'What plan? I live here. I work here. What else can I do? Whatever they hand out I can't see any alternative but to take it as best I can.'

'You can't *what*?' He spun round to look at her so furiously that she looked away. 'You're prepared to let those harpies pull you to pieces? You're prepared to act as if you've committed some outrageous crime and take your punishment?'

His anger completed her demoralisation and she felt tears start at the back of her eyes, tears she had been determined not to shed.

'What do you suggest I do—run off? Where do I run to? What do I do? Even if I could I wouldn't. I live here. I may be an outsider, but I've as much right to be here as they have! They have no right to act like that, and so sneakily! I couldn't come up with one thing to take then to task for other than meanness and they just ignored my reprimands.'

'No, offhand I can't think of a thing you could have done. That sort of attack is a particularly feminine attack and subtle enough to be foolproof. It's like fighting a shadow.'

'You had no trouble,' she choked, and his lips twisted sardonically.

'I'm bigger, a good deal more ferocious, and I don't give a damn.'

'So what do you suggest I do, tackle them one by one daily? Hit them over the head as they enter?'

She realised she was shouting at him and he turned quizzical blue eyes on her.

'Maybe. You seem to have that inclination with me.'

Catrina looked away, temper giving way to misery. It wasn't just the women, the gossip, the unfairness. It was the final realisation that Gary had in effect started this. It might have been his mother who had triggered off the morning's events, but she would not have dared unless he had talked to her, complained to her, told her all about his problems. He knew what she was like. He had told Catrina more than once and told her about his mother's gossiping friends. He must have known what would happen and he had not worried about setting the wolves on her.

'Stop crying,' Zade said harshly. 'It's not going to help.'

'I'm not crying! Just leave me and go!' She raised drenched eyes and shouted at him some more. 'You've helped me. You came and rescued me *again*! I never asked you to. I never asked you to step into my life. I don't want you in it. If I hadn't met you I would never have acted as I did. I would never have known that...'

She suddenly saw his face through a veil of angry tears and realised just what she was saying, how she was raging at him when, if it hadn't been for Zade, she would have been trapped in this cottage with Gary, at his mercy. If it hadn't been for Zade she would probably have finally broken down this morning in front of that pack of horrid women. It was what they wanted.

Zade was taking the blows she was aiming at him with her wild tongue, but his eyes had turned to blue ice and she almost threw herself forward.

'Zade! I'm sorry! I'm sorry!' She dropped to her knees by the chair. 'Please forgive me. If it hadn't been for you I would have been marrying Gary, not knowing how cruel he could be. If it hadn't been for you I would still be in town with those awful women.'

'Oh, I'm sure that temper would have exploded by now,' he said coldly, looking down at her. 'Although they might not have understood that the tears were rage.'

'They're not really,' she confessed, her voice still caught by snatches of tears. 'Please forgive me, Zade.'

For a minute he just looked at her with cold eyes and then he suddenly reached forward and collected her, pulling her up into the chair with him, enclosing her in hard arms and pushing her head to his shoulder.

'You little idiot,' he said, amusement in his voice. 'You're not fighting material. Stop berating both of us. So I keep on rescuing you? What of it? It helps to pass the time.'

'You're very kind to take it so lightly,' Catrina began, wanting to snuggle into the hard warmth, but he lifted her face and looked down at her, capturing her gaze and holding it.

'I'm not kind at all, sugar,' he said softly. 'I live a hard life and I'm hard all the way through.' He went on looking at her and she was once again drowning in the sky. His glance moved over her face, lingering on the thick black lashes, wet with tears, moving over her trembling lips, and then he eased her away from him, standing and putting her on her feet.

'Now that we've got that out of the way,' he said tersely, 'what do you plan to do?'

'I really don't know.' Catrina moved to stand by the fire, looking down into the flames. Her hurt and her temper were gone because for a few minutes she had been lost in Zade's eyes, sinking into them, wanting more. It was difficult to think.

'I can't tell you what to do,' he warned her, pacing about with his hands in his pockets. 'What shall I say? Fight them, cause scenes and force them into the open, or get the hell out of here and go closer to your father? I can't see much future here to fight for and I've never believed in lost causes. Ultimately, though, you decide.'

'I won't even see my father for two weeks,' she said quietly, and Zade stopped pacing.

'Two weeks?'

'He came Saturday night because he was worried about me. He had to do a swap. Now he owes a run to somebody else. I never told him about...about Gary's threat—if it was a threat. I never told him about you.'

'I'm your secret?' he asked drily, and Catrina didn't answer, because in a way that was what Zade was: her secret. She looked away and Zade didn't press the matter. Instead he asked, 'Never mind the long-term plan. What about tomorrow?'

'I'll go back to work. They've got to be faced and, in any case, I have no choice.'

'Of course you have a choice!' He grabbed her arm, spinning her round, glaring at her, and her face went pale.

'Oh, my God!' Zade muttered. 'Why did I have to touch you at all? How did I get myself into this mess!'

He pulled her into his arms almost savagely, but when he felt her instant submission, when he felt the softness of the body, which came so willingly, he covered her mouth with his and there was no savagery at all. He just kissed her deeply and hungrily, gathering her closer as her arms lifted and wound round his neck.

'I know what you need, you black-haired little cat,' he whispered hoarsely against her lips, 'but you're not getting it from me. I'm too busy with my life to be your knight in shining armour and I'm not cut out for it. I'm not a villain either. I go my own lonely way and if I take you I'll leave you.'

Catrina heard the words, but they did not sink into her enchanted mind. This morning's events just faded away and she was swirling down a road of light as his lips came back to hers, probing and hungry. She opened her mouth without any bidding and he groaned deep in his throat as his tongue slid inside, not roughly and insolently as it had done the first time, but slowly and secretly, searching and tasting until her legs just gave way and she clung to him to hold herself up.

'No! No! No!' Zade said hoarsely, putting her from him, pushing her to the chair, and walking away with his hands running through his hair. 'I'm old enough to know better. And I'm not seducing a mixed-up girl who still says she loves somebody who was quite ready to attack her.'

Catrina stared at him blankly. She didn't. She didn't love Gary. She had never really known Gary, not until she had seen him as he had been when he had come here. She had never before looked into his eyes and seen blind rage, a desire to hurt. Gary had almost been a figment of her imagination and she knew he had played a role from the day she had met him. She didn't love Gary at all.

She was not about to tell Zade that, though. She was not about to confess such naïve emotions and see his scorn. He would point out that she was immature, that her affections faded very rapidly. It would not alter anything at all, because this was all desire, chemistry, a sort of magic, but not the magic her father and mother had lived in. That was love.

Catrina jumped up and ran up the stairs, perfectly ready to hide until he left, which he would be doing right now. He did nothing of the sort. He gave her about ten minutes and then called from the bottom of the stairs.

'Catrina! Come down! I'm hungry and so are you. We're going out for lunch.'

She was startled, but she wasn't going anywhere.

'I'm not hungry,' she called back, but it didn't help her at all.

'If I say you're hungry then that's exactly what you are,' he snapped. 'Come down or I come up to get you. Playtime is over and little girls have to be fed.'

Well, that put her in her place, and she scowled at herself in the mirror as she quickly put on lipstick and collected her coat. All right, he could feed her, and after that she would come back, lock herself in, and have a good think. She might just pack a bag and get out of here. From now on it was going to be the worst place in the world and she had the rest of her life to live. She wasn't tied to the place with rope!

After deep consideration she decided she would rather be penniless and sleep under a bridge than be here, because when Zade left she would be fighting on her own and, in any case, he had said he was not a knight in shining armour. He could get on his horse and gallop off! She came down with a scowl on her face and Zade just looked at her with raised brows and ushered her to the door.

This time he took her well away from town. She knew it was solely for her benefit. Left to himself, Zade would have ignored everyone and eaten exactly where he chose, possibly in the market square under a spotlight, but she did not have that kind of self-knowledge. They went to a country inn that was warm, dimly lit and quiet.

'Come to your senses?' Zade asked quizzically when they had almost finished the good, simple food.

'I'm going to run off,' Catrina said petulantly. 'Why should I bother? They can do without a librarian! I'm going to leave without notice, lock up the cottage, and go. I'm going to abscond.'

Zade began to laugh softly, his eyes dancing when she looked up at him in vexation.

'What about relatives? Where are you running to? Where will you sleep tomorrow night? How will you earn a living? How will your father get in touch with you? Have you thought about joining the Foreign Legion?'

'Oh, shut up!' Catrina snapped, staring at him crossly. 'Anyway,' she sighed, suddenly going from petulance to more realistic worry, 'I'll probably have to go back for a while, even if I leave later. I'll have to work out my notice, get another job—and then there's the cottage.'

'You face what you want to face, nothing more,' Zade said seriously, reaching over to grasp her hand. 'You have nothing to prove to anyone. You made a decision about Gary. It concerns the two of you only.'

'What do you think about it?' Catrina asked tremulously, wishing he would move his hand. It was big enough to engulf her slender fingers and warm enough to send waves of relaxation right through her.

'Me? I'm just an interested bystander.' His eyes were where hers were, on their joined hands, and he suddenly straightened up, moving his hand and looking out of the window. 'I just happened to be here. Sheer chance. I had never intended to come again.'

'You weren't going to visit England any more? What made you come?' Suddenly Catrina's heart seemed to sink. She had a vivid picture of how things would have been if Zade had not decided to come. The most vivid thought was that she would never have seen him, never have known him.

'I had something to do,' he informed her tightly. 'One last thing—a duty.'

He just sank into silence and he was still almost silent as they went back to the cottage. He obviously had no intention of staying. He walked with her up the path and Catrina didn't quite know what to do. She should invite him in because he had given her lunch, rescued her, and put up with her burst of weeping and rage. She should also invite him in because she very much wanted to, but he was already too involved and he had said he was merely a bystander. She could not cling to Zade even though the inclination was there.

As they got to the door she glanced up at him and he looked back steadily.

'Do I come in and offer further fatherly advice or do I get the boot?' he enquired drily.

'I—I'd like you to come in,' Catrina confessed, flushing under the probing stare. 'You don't have to, though. I mean, I know it's no concern of yours and I've more or less dragged you into things and——'

'Open the door, Catrina,' he ordered softly. 'I never noticed myself being dragged into anything at all.'

Inside she didn't quite know how to behave. In spite of everything, it wasn't as if Zade was a friend she could chatter to. She was too aware of him to be really at ease. He wandered into the sitting-room as she went to put her coat away and she lingered a little because she had to face him and it was worrying.

The loud knocking on the door startled her. It was almost violent and her heart began to hammer at once.

Inside she knew who it was, although she had not expected it, especially not so soon.

When she reluctantly opened the door, Gary stood there, and he was almost raging. Before she could stop him, he was inside, very close and glaring down at her.

'So we've really got down to the truth,' he snarled. 'You're with Zade! You walked out of the library with him and his car's outside this place now. I must have been blind! You spun me a tale about not marrying me for my own good and all the time you had your eye on Zade. What is it, a ranch instead of a farm? More money? More glamour?'

'More protection,' a cold voice said from the sitting-room doorway, and Catrina could tell from the look on his face that although Gary had seen the car his temper had not even let him follow the thought through, because he was stiff with surprise to see Zade actually there.

'You set out to get her from me! That's what you intended right from the start,' he raged, too angry to see the danger in the blue eyes. 'You've spent more time here than you have at the farm.'

'Get your head examined!' Zade snapped. 'You've frightened her out of her wits. All I've done is rescue her.'

'She wouldn't have needed rescuing if she hadn't turned me down,' Gary bit out. His face was red with rage and Catrina could see he had completely lost control of himself. She wanted to back away, but she dared not move in case it precipitated more violence.

'So you and your kindly mother turned those harridans on her? What was that supposed to achieve? You were going to bring her to her senses?'

'I'm taking the blame for everything, am I?' He turned on Catrina with blazing eyes. 'What tale have you been spinning him, you little . . . ?' He stepped even closer, his fists bunched, and Zade's voice cracked out like an icy whip.

'Don't let it enter your mind. I've got a short fuse and it's lit!'

Gary stepped back, but he was not entirely under control. From rage he suddenly went to vicious amusement.

'A lot of good she'll do you. I had to get my entertainment elsewhere while I was engaged to her. I can wait. You'll be going. She'll see things my way finally. I'll send you an invitation to the wedding.'

'I think she's got more taste than to be the bride,' Zade said coldly. He crossed the hall and opened the door wider. 'Out!' he ordered. 'Make whatever plans you like, but just keep it at the top of your mind that I haven't gone yet.'

On the path, Gary turned and looked at Catrina. Her face was deadly pale and he could see the fright. Evidently he enjoyed seeing it.

'Maybe I'll be back tonight,' he said maliciously. 'Keep the light on, then I'll know you're awake and waiting.'

'She'll be asleep,' Zade warned menacingly. 'So will I, but don't come closer than the gate. I sleep lightly.'

Gary's face dropped into a sort of frozen mask. He looked at Zade with almost panic-stricken disbelief. He said nothing else and as he got to the gate Zade closed the door with very deliberate quietness. His face too was a mask, but it was cold, hard anger.

Catrina was too shocked to move. In the last week she had run through more emotions than she had used in the whole of her life. She had never faced violence before this week. Her life had been surrounded by the love of her parents. She had never faced quarrels, let alone blind, mad rage. She had never been drowned in desire nor seen her life slipping away from her fingers. It had been one shock after another and now she was immobile, blank with the wicked bombardment of Gary's tongue.

Zade pointed to the sitting-room.

'Inside,' he ordered. 'Let's see if you've got the stamina to make it to a chair.'

She just turned like a wooden doll and walked ahead of him, but his voice followed her.

'No tears! What you need is outrage, because you've just been insulted as you've never been insulted in your life.'

'Should I have slapped his face?' Catrina whispered, sitting down and just staring ahead at the fire. Zade had asked her why she hadn't done that when he had first touched her skin.

'Not unless you wanted to see him strangled,' Zade rasped. 'He would have hit you back. He's blown his lid.'

'He'll come back!' Catrina looked up at Zade as he stood by the fire.

'Not while my car's here,' he corrected calmly, 'and my car's not moving.'

'What do you mean?' She couldn't think a car would give her a lot of protection. If Zade left it here and went by taxi Gary could easily find out that Zade was back at his hotel simply by ringing Reception.

'I mean I'm staying.'

'But... but you can't. People will——'

'I should imagine people already have,' he interrupted sardonically. 'However, it's none of their business. Either you come with me and book in at the hotel or I stay here all night. I imagine your father sleeps in a bed? I'm not too fussy. I'll borrow it.'

CHAPTER SIX

DURING the latter part of the afternoon, Zade went back to his hotel. He needed things for the night and he left Catrina with strict instructions to lock up and not answer the door until she saw his car come back. She bit her lips together and nodded. It was so dramatic, almost unbelievable, but when he had gone the silent house alarmed her.

Such a short time ago she had been all set to be Gary's wife, ready to face his mother, life on a farm, and anything else that was needed. She had called him her dearest friend and now she didn't know him at all. She knew Zade. He was like a protective wall around her, and this was the man she had feared on sight. This was the man who had alarmed her with brilliant blue eyes.

Nothing seemed quite real and she was still facing the problem of close proximity to Zade as well as her other problems. It had not gone away, this need to look into his eyes and be swallowed up. She would have to live through it, but tomorrow the same problems would face her. Zade could not stay here indefinitely, protecting her. He would not want to.

She went up to make her father's room ready for him, wondering how she was going to sleep, with Zade just along the passage. She had enough sense to know that if he was not here she would not be sleeping at all. Gary's threat might have been merely a malicious desire to alarm her, but he had succeeded extremely well. Even with Zade here she would be listening until dawn broke.

Zade insisted that they eat out at dinnertime and Catrina readily agreed. No matter who they met and what the looks said that came their way, it was better than simply staying in. She didn't like the idea of facing an evening alone with Zade. He would probably ignore her and she would not be able to ignore him. What would they do, play cards? He would act as if he were baby-sitting.

They ate at the Golden Calf because Zade was not the hiding type. He would probably prefer to take a few townsfolk by the collar and shake a bit of sense into them. He ordered dinner and ignored the other diners.

They did not ignore him, nor did they ignore Catrina. This place was popular and tonight it seemed more popular than ever, and it was no surprise to Catrina at all. They knew where Zade Mackensie was staying and, even if they hadn't, Gary's mother would have enlightened her friends. The information would have been passed along. They wanted a close look at him.

News travelled fast in this dale, and gossip travelled even faster, and by now the whole town would know that the library had been closed this morning in a dramatic way. The Golden Calf was full of interested people who could hardly eat for watching them.

Catrina was glad to escape at the end of it, but she was angry. They had no right to pry into her affairs. She had lived here for six years, but she had never quite become accustomed to the often malicious gossip that filled the lives of some of the people. Now she was at the receiving end herself and as they left she looked round the dining-room very grimly, meeting their prying eyes and staring them down with furious looks.

'Round one to you, I think, Miss Arnold,' Zade murmured as they got to the door. 'Are you going for the knock-out or are you about to retire from the fight?'

Catrina knew she would be retiring from the fight. It was much too one-sided. Her courage would not have been so strong if Zade had not been with her and when he went she just wanted to go too—anywhere. She was no longer part of the community. She was no longer interested in the dale.

The rest of the evening Catrina simply pottered around doing odd jobs that would keep her out of the sitting-room. Zade had brought a book with him and he sat reading it and ignoring her. The silence seemed to be shouting at her and she knew how he felt. He was a guard and he was guarding her from his own cousin. She was a burden to him, a stranger who was imposing on his gallantry. He might say he was not a knight in shining armour, but to her he was.

The guilt of it would have kept her awake even if nerves hadn't, and for ages she paced about her room. She was also weighed down with the guilt of not having spoken to him unless it was necessary. Why couldn't she have simply behaved normally, gossiped about it, raged about it? She knew why. Zade would have listened patiently, but by now he was quite probably bored with the whole thing and wanting to get back to America speedily.

She was also turning the problem of tomorrow around in her mind. She just didn't want to go back to town, back to her job. It would be letting people down, but they deserved it. Those who didn't would just have to blame the others. It still didn't solve the predicament of what she was going to do. She finally put on her dressing-gown and went down the stairs. She couldn't sleep. She would make a drink and read until morning.

She was still in the kitchen, thinking deeply, when Zade suddenly appeared in the doorway, startling her and making her jump.

'What's wrong?' he asked quietly, his eyes alert on her face.

'I just couldn't sleep. I'm sorry if I woke you. I tried to creep about.'

'Maybe it's the creeping about that did it,' he suggested wryly. 'Anyway, I wasn't asleep.'

Catrina tried not to look at him. He had slipped on some jeans to come down. His feet were bare and so was his chest. He was so completely masculine that he took her breath away and her blushes increased when she realised that until she had met Zade any masculine beauty had not even made her raise her eyebrows. She had been quite content with her lack of feeling.

Now she wanted to stand and look at him, let her hands run over the broad, hard chest, let her fingers drift along the powerful muscles, the light covering of hair. He was so tall, so tanned, and there was no difference between the brown of his arms and the brown of his chest.

She looked up, terrified at where her thoughts were going, and he was leaning against the door, watching her.

'I often work with my shirt off,' he said quietly, and she looked away frantically, wondering how much he had seen in her eyes. She was almost breathless, her heart racing, and she searched around for something to say.

'I . . . I'm sorry I didn't talk to you all evening,' she murmured in a small voice, forcing the words past a dry, tight throat. 'I . . . I hope I didn't make you feel annoyed because—because you've been very good to me.'

'You didn't make me feel annoyed,' he told her softly. 'Sitting by the fire talking would not have been a very good idea, would it?'

'Well, I . . . I'm glad you think so. I . . . I'll go back to bed.'

She knew she had to get past him and she kept her head down, feeling she had to almost run, looking up in panic when he didn't move aside. He looked down, holding her gaze with dazzling blue eyes, and when she stood almost rooted to the spot his gaze ran slowly over her face.

'I wasn't really reading. I was thinking.' He lifted his hand and stroked down her cheek gently. 'I was thinking about this.'

She started to move his hand away, realising the danger, but his fingers closed round hers, pulling her hand to his chest and holding it there.

'Are you going to run away?' he asked softly, and she knew she could not, didn't want to. In such a short time, Zade had become necessary to her existence. She had planned to be married, to spend her life with someone she really didn't know. It was Zade she knew, Zade she wanted to be with always. It was what the battle had been about all this time. It was what the magic had been about.

Catrina's breath seemed to be coming in great, heavy sighs, soundless, painful breaths that helped to magnify the weak feeling in her legs. She looked up into his face, but his eyes were moving over her cheeks, her neck, the black shine of her curls, and then his hand curved round her nape, drawing her towards him.

'Don't run, Catrina,' he murmured.

She didn't resist. There was just the silent house, the warm kitchen, the darkened hall and Zade's persuasive fingers, warm and hard beneath her hair, drawing her forward. His fingers trapped a handful of curls, tightening, forcing her face to his, and she closed her eyes and submitted, opening her lips to his demanding mouth, falling into his arms willingly.

Catrina felt herself being drawn up against his body as his arm came tightly round her and then he captured her face, curving his hand around it, sliding his fingers into her hair and kissing her hungrily. She moved closer, instinctively pressing herself against him, and his hand moved to her neck, probing beneath the thick dressing-gown until it encountered her warm skin.

She gave a small, gasping cry, but her breasts surged outwards, full and swollen, and when his hand searched insistently she moved to accommodate him, moaning when his fingers found their objective, his harsh gasp showing his pleasure. He pulled her to his shoulder, his lips never leaving hers, his hand caressing the silken weight of her breast until she was kissing him back urgently, her arm tightly around his neck.

When she was sobbing against his mouth, drowning in excitement, he drew his head back and looked down at her.

'Slowly, gently, little cat,' he ordered thickly. 'You've never felt this before and there's all the time in the world.' His eyes ran over her, watching her bewitched expression, seeing her enchantment, and his face was dark, sensuous, with a hard passion in his eyes that should have frightened her.

It didn't. She reached fervently for his lips, but he slid his mouth over hers and then nibbled at her ear, running his tongue round it, bringing shivers to her whole body. He tightened her to him and she felt the hard evidence of masculine desire for the first time ever. She had not allowed anyone to hold her so close before, even her own fiancé, but she couldn't get close enough to Zade.

She softened against him, moving with rapture into the hardening planes of his body, and he bit painfully at her earlobe.

'I want you, Catrina,' he whispered. 'Tonight I'm going to teach you what pleasure is all about.'

He lifted her into his arms and walked through to the darkened sitting-room, where the fire still burned brightly, throwing dancing shadows on the walls, and he turned her face against the power of his chest, delighting in the abrasive feel of the hair against her cheek.

She placed her hand against the heavy beat of his heart and raised herself up to touch his shoulder with the tip of her tongue, excited when a shudder raced through him.

Zade put her on her feet by the fire and cupped her face in his hands, looking down at her with glittering eyes.

'Slowly, baby,' he ordered thickly. 'I've only got so much control. I'm not a superman. I don't want you hurt.'

Catrina never thought about being hurt and when he unfastened her dressing-gown and dropped it on the settee she just watched him with wide, glowing eyes, her cheeks flushed and her heart racing. Even when he slipped the small buttons at the neck of her nightie and began to ease it from her she could only look at him. His face was taut with desire as he slowly uncovered her and as the nightie slid to the carpet he claimed her mouth with his and drew her down to the thick rug in front of the fire.

'You're beautiful,' he murmured huskily against her lips. 'Warm and willing, silky as a kitten, and all burned up inside.' He began to kiss her face, fierce little kisses that made her skin grow hot. 'Are you burning inside Catrina?' he asked between swift, heated kisses. 'Are you burning up for me?'

Catrina didn't want to talk. She was rushing into the magic, the fire she had always denied racing through her blood. She tried to draw his mouth back to hers and he came to her with a shaken laugh, pulling her against him and running his hands over her with fierce pleasure. She pressed herself against him even more, impatient with the rough touch of jeans, wanting his skin against hers, whimpering in distress, and Zade looked down into her dark, dazed eyes.

'Yes,' he said thickly. 'Anything you want, sweet-heart, anything at all.'

He shrugged out of his jeans without moving from her, his hands still bringing singing pleasure to her skin, and Catrina gasped as he returned to her fiercely, moving over her and pressing her down into the rug, sleek and strong, hard, powerful muscles against her softly feminine body.

His strength didn't frighten her. She had been a long way past fear as soon as he touched her in the kitchen and now she yearned against him, her lips as heated as his, her body twisting against him frantically until his kisses hardened and his hands found every nerve-ending, every secret place. Her small cries of pleasure drove him further. His lips found her breasts, teasing urgently, sending pain and excitement down to her toes, making her toss wildly beneath him.

Catrina kissed him fiercely too, no knowledge of what to do except the driving need inside her that told her. She wanted to keep Zade for herself, to be with him always. She wrapped her slender legs around him and his hand ran down her back with possessive compulsion, arching her beneath him, his mouth fusing with hers as he entered her slowly and strongly.

She gave a wild cry of pain, but the pressure didn't ease and she pressed herself against him, accepting the fire, sinking into it, closing around him, trapping him in delight.

He gave a low growl deep in his throat, moving inside her and building up the fierce heat and pleasure. 'I've waited for this since I first saw you. These days have been the longest days of my life.'

Catrina had been the one to urge him on; for a few dazzling seconds she had owned Zade, snapped his control, but now she was a weak, yearning creature, gasping beneath his drive to possess her, shaken by the rhythm of his body until the world split into pieces and she fell off the end in his arms.

She lay beneath him in the darkening room, her heart hammering. She was burned up by her own fire and Zade's, her body weak with pleasure. He lay heavily against her, his breathing harsh, uneven, his hands still moving over her, and she had no thoughts at all in her mind. Since she had met him she had been drowning in his eyes; now she was floating, spent, without thought. She was just part of Zade and she knew exactly what her father had meant. She had felt the perfect magic. She loved Zade.

It bewitched her and she lay limp and dazed. She had never seen it coming until tonight when she had seen him. The heat she had sought was something she had never experienced. Zade had fused it all together. She never wanted to move from him.

After a minute he eased his weight away and looked down at her. She was surprised that she could meet the brilliant eyes and she looked back with no shyness. He was part of her, her other self. His mind probed into hers and then he rested on one elbow and regarded her with a quizzical smile on his lips.

'Did you really want a drink?' he asked softly. She shook her head slowly, never taking her eyes from him, and he stood with one lithe movement and pulled her to her feet. When she swayed dizzily, he caught her against him, bending to collect their clothes and push them into her hands.

'Then we'll go to bed,' he said quietly, lifting her into his arms. 'It's a long, long time until morning.'

Zade took her into her own bedroom and she looked at him mournfully when he moved towards the bed. He was going to leave her, leave her without saying anything. He looked down at her and his eyes were serious, intent, searching her face.

'I'm staying with you,' he said huskily. 'Tell me to go if you don't want to sleep with me. I guess I can summon up the necessary courage to walk out of the door and back to your father's room.'

Catrina closed her eyes as he placed her on the bed, but her hands reached out, and he swept aside the clothes that she had carried up with them and she was once again back in hard, demanding arms.

'You've got a lot to learn,' he breathed hungrily against her mouth, 'but there's nothing I can't teach you by morning.'

When Catrina awoke she lay with her eyes closed, almost afraid to open them in case it was nothing but a dream. It was not a dream, though. Her aching, lethargic body told her she was different and her mind seemed to be singing all by itself. She had been in Zade's arms all night, wrapped in hard warmth, heated by his kisses. She could still feel the delight, still hear his voice gently coaxing against her skin. It was the first morning of being in love.

She opened glowing eyes, turning her head to see him, but he was not there, and a brief spell of desolation washed over her until she heard him downstairs. She struggled out of bed, trying to find her watch. It was ten o'clock! Catrina was utterly disorientated. By now she should have been at work, the library open, and she sat on the edge of the bed, remembering other things too. Yesterday she had walked out of the library, propelled by Zade's hard hand. Everything in her life had changed and it was wonderful.

The telephone in the hall rang and she made a hasty dive for her dressing-gown, finding it at the foot of the bed. Zade would come up to get her, to tell her somebody was ringing. Her face flushed at the thought of him finding her as she had awakened, naked and dreamy.

She tied her dressing-gown tightly, running her hand through her thick, short curls and hurrying to the door.

He was not coming to get her. He was standing in the hall answering the phone and she was so hypnotised by him that she stood at the top of the stairs and just watched him. He looked clean, shining, his jeans clinging to strong, long legs, his broad shoulders moving easily under a thin white sweater. It was a second or two before it sank in that he was answering her phone without even calling her.

'Miss Arnold is not well. She will not be in today, probably not tomorrow either.' Catrina just stood listening in stunned silence and he added, 'Surely you have a stand-by? Are you telling me that in the normal course of events none of your staff is unwell?'

His final words were rather typical and brought a smile to Catrina's lips.

'Then I suggest you jump to it right now.'

As he put the phone down he glanced up and saw her and he came to lean against the carved banister post, looking up at her steadily.

'That was your boss. I believe he called himself the chief librarian, although I may be wrong. I wasn't too interested. He wanted to know why the library was closed; apparently he's had complaints.'

'I should have phoned in,' Catrina began, but he gave her a wry look and one of those sardonic smiles.

'You were asleep. In any case, let them cope. The library now has an emergency. You had your emergency yesterday morning. They're reaping the harvest.'

'I'll get the sack.'

'Does it really matter?' He went on looking up at her and she shook her head. No, it really didn't matter. She didn't quite know what she was going to do, but nothing seemed to matter at this moment except looking at Zade.

'Breakfast in three minutes,' he announced. 'Eat as you are or move fast.'

That was when she smelled the toast, the bacon, and Catrina suddenly felt hungry and wildly alive. She turned and rushed back to her room, throwing off her dressing-gown, diving into the bathroom and under the hot shower. It was a wonderful, wonderful day!

When she came down she wasn't too sure about that. Zade was dishing up the breakfast, putting it on the table at the places he had set, and as she sat down he sat opposite and began to eat. He said nothing at all. He didn't even look at her and the rosy glow began to fade from Catrina's cheeks.

She remembered then the words he had said in the afternoon when he had kissed her. He had told her he would leave her, go back to his lonely ways. His long hours of gentle lovemaking did not mean that he loved her too. He had been thrown into her life, forced to help, to offer his protection, and she had brought on all the passion herself. She couldn't expect Zade to feel the same.

They ate in silence until the whole enchantment drained away from her and she was once again shy, tongue-tied with Zade. In the end she forced herself to speak.

'I...I slept a long time.'

He slanted her a look from beneath lowered lids, a dazzling blue look that contained a great deal of irony.

'Not too long—considering.' He sat back and watched the colour flood back into her cheeks. 'I'm an early riser. I have to be. I was up at seven and that's very late for me. I saw no reason to wake you.'

It reminded Catrina rather forcefully that when Zade had awakened he had been beside her. It reminded her too of last night and deep into the night, and she looked down quickly.

'I should have been getting ready for work.'

'You're excused.' His laconic statement brought her eyes back to his and he let his glance drift over her face and along the slightly bruised length of her lips.

'There's tomorrow.'

'That's another day. This one's hardly begun. Things are different,' he said quietly.

Catrina jumped up and started to clear the dishes away. She didn't know what he meant. She was still shaken with the whole wonder of loving him and Zade was back to normal, a cool, hard masculine being with eyes that could see a long way.

'I...I can't see why things are different. I have to plan,' she muttered, filling the sink with water and putting the dishes into it.

'Can't you?' He stood and came to stand beside her. 'Are we going to forget about last night? I'm responsible for you.'

'Nobody is responsible for me,' Catrina said tightly. 'I've been trying to tell you that I'm a perfectly capable adult since I first met you.'

She belonged to him, was totally committed to him, loved him so much that her heart threatened to burst, but she expected nothing at all. It was her own grief that Zade was not enclosed in the magic. There was no reason to change his life.

'Catrina.' He said her name impatiently, took her hands out of the soapy water and held them tightly in his, but she refused to look up and let him see what was in her eyes. Zade had wanted her. Now he felt responsible. It was not what she wanted at all.

The doorbell rang and she looked up then, not knowing now how to act, too shaken by her own feelings to face anyone. Zade simply met her gaze evenly.

'Perhaps this is where you show those capabilities,' he murmured as he walked out of the kitchen and into the hall. He was in charge, as he always seemed to be. He was in charge of her too, but she would never let him know. When she walked into the hall behind him he already had the door open, and Gary was standing there, looking at Zade in utter silence.

'Coming in or staying out?' Zade rasped.

'You've been here all night,' Gary began stormily, and Zade interrupted in a cool voice that allowed no doubts.

'Every minute of it. I cooked breakfast. Want to know what we had?'

'I want to see Trina!' Gary stood like a bull ready to charge and Catrina moved forward, still wanting to soothe because it was habit, something she had always done. She didn't get the chance to speak, though, let alone soothe.

'Come in, then,' Zade grated. 'She's only just got up from a warm bed and it's damned cold in the hall now we've had the door open to chatter.'

It wasn't exactly chatter. It was like the trumpet call before a battle and Catrina's face flushed at Zade's words. With nothing specific he had painted an erotic picture, and it wasn't lost on Gary. He came in, his eyes going from one to the other. For a minute she expected violence, but he controlled himself with a supreme effort and managed a smile when he finally gave all his attention to her.

'I heard about yesterday at the library,' he said quietly. 'I'd no idea why you walked out. I just wanted to know you were all right. They've no business to stick their noses in our affairs.'

It was said as if there had been just a small lovers' tiff and once again Catrina was believing it, doing what she had done since she had known Gary, making excuses for him, believing he hadn't known. Zade watched with cold, hard eyes and there was no doubt that Gary saw her weaken. Zade certainly saw it.

'I know I frightened you with my temper, love,' Gary said softly, taking a step towards her. 'You've got to see, though, that I was hurt. You and I have been planning the wedding for a year. I can't just give you up. I love you.'

Catrina couldn't say a word because she was hearing other words, the words Gary had used when Zade had thrown him out of here. She remembered how cheap he had made her feel, how he had admitted to being with other women while he was engaged to her. She remembered with a shudder of fear his expression as he had planned to drag her into the cottage and settle her future. It made her incapable of speech, because he was doing it again, doing what he had always done, playing her along. Now, however, she recognised it. She just didn't know Gary at all. He was a stranger, a violent stranger.

He took her silence to be acquiescence and, by the look on his face, so did Zade. There was mounting triumph on Gary's face and he came closer.

'I don't care if he's spent the night in the house,' he said more firmly, his security with his own ego restored. 'I certainly know he'll have slept by himself. Who knows that better than me? I can smooth over all the trouble in town. I still want to marry you.'

'Enough to bring up my child?' Zade asked acidly. 'That sure is a lot of loving devotion.'

Gary's head snapped up as if he had taken a blow and his eyes met cold blue as Zade looked down at him.

'That's not true!' he shouted, back to rage immediately, his carefully rehearsed gentleness gone as if it had never been there. 'She wouldn't——'

'Look at her,' Zade rasped, and Catrina knew what he would see. He would see a different person, a woman. So far she had said nothing and now she wasn't even thinking about this. Her mind was swirling around Zade, asking her why he had said that, why he even thought it. And she knew he didn't. He was simply lashing out at his cousin with the same old caustic tongue. He was tightening the leash when he thought she was in danger of softening. It was two male animals locked in battle. Zade was just trying to protect her from what he imagined was her own stupidity.

'You cheating little...!' Gary had seen her expression, read the truth on her face, and he lashed out at her with a wildly swinging arm. It never connected. A hand like steel grasped his wrist, forcing it back slowly and painfully, and Zade stood over him without even appearing to exert any energy.

'Be thankful you missed,' he said menacingly. 'Get it into your head that this place is out of bounds. Catrina gave the ring back. She doesn't want to marry you. She won't even be here.'

He opened the door and propelled Gary outside with no ceremony and Catrina walked back into the warmth of the kitchen, shaking and bewildered, because a new problem had arisen, one she had never even thought of.

When Zade walked in to join her she was staring at him with wide, accusing eyes.

'Why did you say that?' she whispered. 'Why did you even think of it?'

'At least one of us should be capable of thought,' Zade said cuttingly. 'Your thoughts run to forgive and forget. Mine don't!'

'What...what you said to Gary... It's just not possible...'

'Do committed virgins take precautions?' he asked bitingly. 'Or do they simply rely on abstinence?'

Catrina blushed painfully, unable now to meet his eyes. She felt naïve and foolish, blurting out things she knew were not true. She clung to the chance that he was simply angry.

'It was only once.'

'Once at a time,' he corrected derisively. 'If it hasn't happened it's not for want of trying.'

'You ... you thought about it?' Catrina stared up at him, trembling and distressed, because all her wonderful magic had gone and the cold, hard world was looking her in the face as surely as Zade's cold blue eyes were watching her anxiety.

'I thought about it,' he confessed drily. 'It suits me just fine because you're going to get married very soon. You're marrying me.'

Whatever else he had said could not have shocked her as much as that. He didn't love her; she wasn't sure if he even liked her. He had wanted her, but she was even uncertain about that now.

'We don't love each other,' she whispered shakily, immediately on the defensive, and he suddenly smiled down at her grimly, reaching out and pulling her towards him until she was enclosed in hard arms that offered nothing but possession.

'I'm not even certain what love is,' he confessed in ironic amusement. 'It seems to be one of the few things I haven't experienced. I know what I want, though. I want a wife who can burn up in my arms, meet desire with desire. I work hard and live lonely. Now I've got you.'

Catrina felt numb, tricked out of her dazzling happiness.

'You did it deliberately?' There was reproach in her face, in the soft brown eyes that had glowed this morning, and for an instant he tightened his hand in her silken curls, jerking her head up angrily, a look she could not read flashing across his lean, handsome face, but he suddenly relaxed just as she thought he would shout at her.

'Yes. I did it deliberately and you helped all the way along the line. I never noticed you begging for mercy, Catrina.'

'I don't have to marry you.'

'No, you don't. I can't make you marry me. So let's get to that planning session you mentioned. What do you want to do now, stay here with the possibility of pregnancy and carry on as normal? Do you want to do your shopping in town, stay on at the library as long as you can, face the tormentors? Or would you like a nice, lonely flat in London, seeing your father when he's in England, managing by yourself and relying on him for support until you can get in touch with me?'

'Why should I get in touch with you? I . . . I told you I can manage my affairs.'

'Is that what I am—an affair—your first? I'm astonished to find you taking things so blithely. Unfortunately I don't feel the same. If you're pregnant, the baby is mine.'

Catrina just stared at him blankly.

'Why should you care?'

'You want me to put you over my knee and beat you?' he asked angrily. 'You're confusing me with Gary.'

'I feel as if you've deliberately trapped me,' Catrina whispered.

'Maybe I have,' he conceded harshly. 'Just look at it another way, though. You're trapped with me and I can give you what you want—this.'

His head swooped down and he captured her mouth with his, kissing her so possessively, so deeply that she felt every bit of breath leave her body. Within seconds she was trembling, back to magic, remembering last night and more than willing when he began to caress her with hungry hands.

'Oh, yes,' he breathed thickly. 'You're in a trap, Catrina. But you walked willingly into it after a whole lot of begging and you'll stay in it with me because when I leave you leave with me.'

When he finally let her go, Catrina couldn't think of anything but being with him, staying with him, and Zade looked down at her with satisfaction.

'You can resign from the library,' he said quietly. 'You've got another job.'

'What can I do?' she whispered, looking up into his eyes, and he suddenly grinned, back to taunting, lifting her away from him and turning to the door.

'Everything I tell you until you're capable of a bit of fight,' he said wryly. 'I'm going to check out of the hotel and get my things. Your first order is to settle down and think how to get in touch with your father. After that, you can start packing. By evening we want to be out of here and heading down to London. I've only got a limited time in this country. Anyway,' he added sardonically, 'I can do without visits from ex-fiancés, and if my aunt comes to congratulate me I'll just break up inside.'

There was a look of satisfaction about him that Catrina could not believe. If she was trapped then so was he. She was trapped by love, though. Zade had made his own trap and deliberately walked into it. She was no closer to understanding him than she had ever been.

CHAPTER SEVEN

CATRINA felt as if she had been travelling for days, even months. From one plane to another, across the Atlantic, across states. Zade had cared for her, guided her, watched her all the time, as if she were absolutely fragile, but he was now the man she had first met, cool, aloof and distant.

It was almost the end of their journey. The plane was smaller, time running out, and her nerves were tightening with every mile. She had never envisaged this distance, the vast and bewildering time-scale. She rested her head and thought of the days in England when she had taken the decision to come with Zade and altered her whole life.

Catrina had known she could not get in touch with her father, at least not to speak to him. She had a number to ring, however, and they told her he would be back in two days—a very short stop, but he would actually be in London. She was able to leave a message. She simply asked him to get in touch when he arrived. When he came in for just a small stop he stayed in London. If he was not using a hotel he stayed with friends. They were people that the whole family had known well at one time, people she had now lost touch with. Her father had not lost touch, though, and she knew that, even after six years, he really felt more at home in the south than up the dale.

What would he say? What would he do now? They were going to be separated by thousands of miles. He would retire all too soon and then he would have nobody

115

but friends from their past. Leaving him behind would be terrible and she knew it. But how could she stay? If Zade's speculations came true she would be entirely dependent on her father for a considerable time. If she had not loved Zade so much she would perhaps have risked it, but she knew deep inside that if he left and she never saw him again she would be torn in two.

She wanted to be with Zade, wanted simply to follow him, and he wanted her, wanted her enough to marry her, enough to have even planned to force her into going with him. He needed a wife and the thought that it would only be desire was bleak, but it was better than never seeing him again, because she knew that after this he would never come back to England. There was nothing to bring him here.

When he came back from his hotel she was packing. She had no idea what she would be facing, but she took everything she had. Her cases were on the bed when Zade returned and he came straight up the stairs to look for her. He stood at the door and watched for a minute, saying nothing, and Catrina was back to shyness, well aware that the man standing tall and silent was still a stranger.

'Want any help?' he asked when she didn't speak.

'I can manage so far. I . . . I'm not sure what to take. I'm taking all my clothes, but——'

'You can take what you want. I suggest you give a lot of thought to anything you're attached to. It's a long way to Montana and there's no coming back.'

His tone made her raise her head sharply, her eyes seeking his, and he was looking at her intently, almost suspiciously, as if she was about to run away and ignore everything.

'I'm surprised to see you so busy, packing so methodically. So far, I've done all the talking and you've said nothing, not even before I left. I want the words, Catrina, a commitment. Are you going to marry me?'

'Yes.' She stood quite still, a dress in her hands already folded. It was on the tip of her tongue to add that she loved him and couldn't even think of seeing him go, but his all-seeing blue eyes dominated her and at this moment he looked hard, self-sufficient, and not in need of loving words. 'I couldn't stay here in any case. My life in this town has just fallen apart. I can't stay with my father either, because if...if... He's retiring soon and I wouldn't want to burden him with my problems.'

'Maybe he'd rather have you as a burden than not have you at all,' Zade said in a cold voice.

'He would; that's why I can't do it to him.' She twisted the dress anxiously. 'If you've changed your mind...if you don't want me to——'

'I've not changed my mind,' Zade said quietly. 'My mind was made up the moment I saw you. You had every chance to freeze me out and stay with Gary, but you came to me. We both wanted you and I've got you. We'll be married before we leave London.'

He turned and went down the stairs and Catrina continued packing, slowly, methodically, keeping her mind off the future. It seemed to be a hard future. Zade had promised nothing at all except marriage. She had walked right into it, drawn by a power she had felt when she had first seen him, and now the rest of her life was in his hands. It could be magic or it could be cold. Zade would set the pace.

Her father flew in two days later and by that time they had established themselves in a hotel and Zade had set about arranging the wedding, her papers and every other thing she would need to go with him. He had also taken her shopping, making sure she had everything she would need, and Catrina was reeling from it all. He was like a dynamo, almost brutally efficient, and it seemed that

every word they spoke to each other was businesslike
plans and arrangements that she was just moved throug
with a bewildered speed.

Zade booked two rooms and never attempted to touc
her. By the time her father came she was utterly be
mused and Zade was even more of a stranger. Inside sl
was beginning to be frightened and only looking at Zad
steadied her. It reminded her that if she backed out of
this she would never see him again and it was enoug
to drive her on each day. When her father phoned sl
was almost in tears, the sound of his voice somethir
to hang on to, and he heard it very clearly.

'Tell me where you are,' he ordered. 'I'll be with yo
in fifteen minutes.'

Zade left her to see him alone. She couldn't deci
whether it was kindness or indifference, but it gave h
the chance to talk without piercing eyes on her. Whe
she told her father she was marrying Zade he was co
pletely silent.

'You don't know him,' he reminded her. He had li
tened to everything that had happened in almost col
plete silence and he didn't criticise her actions in keepi
it from him before. He knew that Zade had rescued he
that Zade was Gary's cousin. Only the very private thir
between herself and Zade were kept from him.

'How well did you know my mother?' Catrina ask
seriously.

'You're hitting below the belt, Cat,' he pointed o
'It was different.'

'You mean it was magic? It's magic for me, Dad.'

'And Zade? What is it for Zade?' He looked at h
closely and she couldn't lie.

'I don't know. It's something I'll have to find out

He tried to talk her out of it, asking her to wait, b
there was no waiting with Zade. He was driving thir

on ruthlessly and he would be going home. She would not get a second chance.

When her father met Zade it was like two giants meeting, summing each other up. Zade deferred to her father's age, but that was all. The clear blue eyes watched, assessed and decided. Her father seemed to have decided too, because he suddenly smiled.

'Have it your own way, love,' he told Catrina quietly. 'You know I'll be here.'

That struck at her conscience and she bit her lip anxiously.

'What are you going to do—about the cottage, I mean?'

'Sell it. I like the south. My memories are here and my friends. Your mother and I were happy here for a long, long time. When I retire I don't want it to be to a bleak dale with bad winters and worse gossips.'

'You could come to us,' Zade offered quietly. 'There's plenty of room at the ranch and Montana is a big place, big enough for both of us,' he added with a slow smile.

'I might do that, once in a while.'

Catrina looked from one to the other, both big men, the only men in her life. They liked each other. She could see that and it made her fleetingly happy. What the future would bring she did not know, but from this moment the past was behind her.

It was certainly behind her now. They were in a light plane and it was possible for the first time to see below. Zade had told her they were now flying over his home state and she looked down to see the vast, rolling plains of Montana. In the distance now were mountains, foothills and outcrops of the mightier Rocky Mountains that stretched from Canada and cut through the state. There were rounded hills, sharp ridges, and over everything the snow lay white and cold. At the moment it looked bleak, uncompromising and, to her English

mind, a limitless, unrelenting landscape. Several time
the main state highways slashed across the land, but sh
saw few towns and the endless vista of snow and dis
tance dazzled her eyes.

'I didn't think there would be snow,' Catrina mur
mured, glancing at Zade as he sat beside her, uncor
cernedly reading a paper he had picked up at the las
stop. 'It's April.'

'It tends to hang on a bit here,' he informed he:
glancing at her rather awe-stricken face. 'We sometime
get an April blizzard that can wipe out any new calves
mature stock too if we're not quick off the mark. It take
some watching.' He went back to reading and Catrin
bit at her lip, wondering what this new life would t
like. Without Zade, it would be lonely; she knew tha
Maybe it would be lonely even with Zade because
looked different now, a cattleman, calm and silent lil
others she had seen as they changed to this light plan

In a little while, he folded his paper and glanced dow
at the white, rolling landscape.

'Time to get ready. Just a few more minutes.'

He reached up and handed her one of the jackets
had bought for her in London. It was thick, light a
warm, and at the time she had thought it a bit too warr
but now she could see the need for it and wondered hc
this land would be in deep winter.

Zade shrugged into his jacket and as she looked dov
the darker shapes and faint lights of a town becan
visible, ever closer as the plane approached. Catrin
heart started to thump heavily. They were arriving.
was her new life. There were new people to meet—Zad
mother and stepfather most particularly. People mig
look with great surprise at Zade's new bride, a librari
from a small, obscure dale in England who had co
to face this vast land and cope with a life married tc

cool, strong man who thought a great deal, but said very little.

She took a deep breath and raised her chin firmly. Zade's mother had come here from the same dale and she had coped. Whatever his reasons, Zade had wanted to marry her, wanted her here, and time would tell how much. She glanced at him and he was watching her intently, his eyes narrowed on her face.

'Scared?' he asked softly.

'Not exactly,' Catrina assured him firmly, her brown eyes sparkling with a flash of temper at his almost menacing query. 'Slightly apprehensive, perhaps, but that's nothing unusual, surely, after such a long trip? I imagine that by morning I'll be quite normal, whatever that is.'

She got the benefit of a slow smile as his eyes bored into hers.

'That's good to hear,' he drawled. 'Let's hope you're right. It's a bit far to consider scooting back.'

'You said there would be no going back,' Catrina reminded him quietly, but he wasn't really listening any more; all she got was a grunt of agreement. Zade was peering through the window, scanning the area around the sheds as the plane landed and taxied forward. He sat back as his eyes saw what they had been searching for.

'Well, that's a relief,' he said. 'Bart had the car brought over. Now you won't have to walk to the ranch.'

After that, Catrina was too busily occupied to be scared. Their luggage was offloaded and it seemed to have grown even more since they had left England. Zade brought the car up, a huge American car that looked roomy and tough, a station wagon of a type she did not know. She was too busy keeping warm to really study it, thankful to snuggle into the hood of her jacket, blessing the high leather boots and the bright cords she had worn at Zade's insistence. The cold evening was swiftly falling, a few bright stars overhead chilly and glittering in the frosty air.

Even when they had pulled away, the car easily swallowing their luggage, Zade seemed to be alert, glancing round at the darkening sheds and only sitting back as they skirted the town and headed south on the main highway. He was making Catrina more edgy every minute and he suddenly seemed to realise it.

'No problem,' he told her with a grin. 'I was half expecting a noisy welcoming committee. The boys are a bit frisky when they're at a loose end. Normally they just groan when I get back, but a new wife is something again.'

She assumed he meant the ranch hands and she was glad there had been no welcoming party.

'They're at loose end?'

'More than likely,' Zade muttered. 'They won't be tomorrow morning.' He didn't look grim. He was just stating a fact. He was the boss and he was back. He looked satisfied about that, eager to be out on the wide acres of the ranch, and Catrina wondered just what she was going to do. She had never asked Zade, never wondered about her duties as his wife. It would be very, very different from anything she had known, and for the first time she wondered if she would be up to it.

It seemed a long time before they turned off the main road and then it was on to another road, a straight, narrow road that headed for the low range of mountains. The sharp ridges seemed closer now, black against the darkening sky, high, wild stars glittering above them. They were going into a wilderness, the great, sweeping land of rolling hills and gullies snow-covered around them. There were clumps of trees, leafless and stark against the sky, others the tall, graceful firs with snow hanging from them like giant Christmas trees.

Fences appeared, stretching in a never-ending line across the glistening white, and then, as the car bumped over a huge cattle-grid, Catrina looked up and saw the great, curving sign that spanned the road from side to side high overhead. Even in the gathering dusk the words were clear, black and huge, big enough to read at speed. 'Mackensie Ranch'. She was home, but it didn't feel like that, because one glance at Zade told her he felt nothing at all but some deep, underlying satisfaction that curved the hard, firm lips into a near smile.

The ranch complex was almost like a small village, much bigger than Catrina had expected. It stood on a tree-dotted rise, rolling hills behind it, the sheds and sturdy buildings clear of the main house. It was the house that drew Catrina's gaze, though, because from now on it was her home and she wanted to look at it intently.

She had thought about it frequently on her long journey here, but never actually imagined it as it was. The ranch house was, as Zade had once said sardonically, not a wooden hut he had built himself. It was low, big and attractive, spreading across the top of the rise, with stands of Douglas fir black against the sky, protecting it from the wind.

The lower half was stone, worn smooth with the years, mellowed and coloured against the dark wood that completed the height. The roof was steep, sharply tilted to withstand snow, and everything seemed to welcome her, from the smoke curling at the chimney to the windows flushed with light. Behind it, the sky proclaimed the end of the day, night clouds like dark satin closing down the last strips of evening sky, and Catrina felt a sudden burst of enchantment, the cold air forgotten.

She just sat and stared as the car stopped by the shallow steps to the door and Zade turned to look at her, watching her for a second, his arm along the back of the seat. As she turned her head to look at him, his hand slid round her face, tilting it towards his.

'You're home, Mrs Mackensie,' he said softly. Before she could make any comment, his mouth captured hers and his fingers slid into her hair as he drew her close. It was the first time he had touched her for days and it brought a great, leaping happiness as she willingly moved against him, relaxing from all the tension when his arms came round her. Zade did want her after all. His lips were warm and coaxing, his hand against her face possessive, and she kissed him back with growing pleasure.

She was flushed and breathless when he lifted his head and the fact that he said nothing at all didn't drive the enchantment away. He got out and came round for her, helping her out and flicking down the hood of her jacket, but he didn't look at her. He just led her into the house, into the bright light and the warmth. Funnily enough, she had never thought at all about her change of name until he had said it. She was Catrina Mackensie now, another being, the wife of the tall, tough man who walked beside her.

Happiness was trying to bubble to the surface. It was a little too soon to let it loose, though, but her eyes were shining, warm and brown, and Zade looked down at her, his eyes flashing over her black, tossing curls, her flushed cheeks and the soft, sweet curve of her mouth.

'An English bride with tinted skin and black curls,' he mused. His lips tilted in a wry smile. 'I wonder what they're going to make of you?' He led her across the shining wooden floor of the hall, his hand on her arm.

'We'll get you warmed up,' he said, making for large double doors that were tightly closed. 'I noticed there was a fire and it's in here.'

He flung the doors open and there was not just a fire burning brightly in a huge fireplace; there was light from lamps, light glittering on glasses, and there was uproar.

The room seemed to be packed with people, people who had been utterly silent as Catrina and Zade had arrived. Now they burst into sound, shouting, cheering and whooping, taking Zade completely by surprise and shaking Catrina out of her wits. For a long time she had been in silence, the silence of the landscape, the silence of the man who sat beside her. Now she was in a whirl of loud noise that confused her and made her suddenly cling to Zade's arm.

When she looked up, Zade was laughing. He glanced at her stunned face and put his arm around her tightly. It seemed to be a signal for the end of the noise because suddenly they were silent again and Catrina found herself facing a sea of grinning faces and more interested eyes than she had ever seen. Every eye was on her, too, and she found it difficult to smile back after such a shock.

'Don't let them scare you, honey,' Zade drawled in amusement. 'They're only at a loose end—until to-morrow morning.'

Most of the visitors were men and several of them groaned theatrically at this, and then Catrina was facing the two people she had most wanted to see, as a big man, tall as Zade, but white-haired, came forward with a slim, greying woman who was Zade's mother.

'Might have known he'd have to go back there to find a wife,' Bart Mackensie growled good-humouredly. 'Nobody here can stand him for long. You've made a big mistake, girlie; he never stops working.'

'I expect she'll cope. I had to,' Zade's mother pointed out with a wide, friendly smile. She hugged Catrina and then stood back to have a close look at her. 'Well, he went back to his roots to find a wife. It might be flattering, but somehow I don't see the dales in you.'

'My mother was Italian,' Catrina said quietly. 'We only moved to the dales six years ago.'

'Ah! An outsider?' Jean Mackensie gave a little laugh, her smile widening when Zade grunted,

'And how! Things don't change much there. I whisked her away right from under their noses.'

'Before she knew what she was letting herself in for?' a voice drawled coolly, and Catrina looked up to find herself being closely observed by green eyes that had only the faintest cover of friendliness over the hard stare. The woman was taller than Catrina, brown as Zade, slim, athletic-looking, and seemed in some way to be part of the place. She was in jeans and a checked shirt and Catrina could see that, whatever her own future, this woman fitted in here. She was like Zade.

'Stella Cunningham,' Zade introduced laconically. 'You'd better take note of her, Catrina—she's part of the landscape, not too easy to ignore.'

'I aim to stay part of the landscape,' Stella Cunningham retaliated with a flashing look at Zade. 'I hope you can manage out here, Catrina. Being permanent in these parts can be hard.'

'Marriage is permanent,' Zade said with a sudden chill in his voice.

'In this day and age?' Stella slanted a look at him that was a challenge, a head-on attack. 'Suppose Catrina can't stand the emptiness, the distances?'

Zade's reply was unexpected. From obvious annoyance he softened, attacking from another angle entirely. His arm came around Catrina's shoulders and he tilted her flushed face with the back of his hand, looking down at her with piercing eyes.

'Thinking of leaving me, Catrina?' he enquired softly. Instantly she was gripped by the dazzling blue of his eyes, lost in the power he used so effortlessly, and her voice was almost husky.

'No. I'm stuck with you permanently.'

She wasn't sure what she should have said, but Zade appeared to be satisfied, and Stella gave a little grunt of annoyance before disappearing into the crowd of people who were already drinking to the bride and groom and seemed to have missed the small battle. There was a momentary flare of anger in Zade's eyes, but he clamped down on it, and Catrina found herself almost torn from him by his mother as Bart Mackensie began a long and detailed report on the happenings at the ranch while Zade had been away.

'Leave them to it,' Jean Mackensie said firmly, leading her off. 'Bart will ignore the fact that you've both been travelling for ages; so will Zade. It's the ranch first and foremost always.'

'I suppose I'll get used to that,' Catrina mused, managing a smile. She was still thinking about that exchange with Stella. Somehow she had not imagined a woman in Zade's life. He had said his life was a lonely one and she had believed it. Stella Cunningham was not pleased to see him married, though, and there was a battle of some sorts raging between them.

'I got used to it,' Jean Mackensie pointed out. 'It's a good life and Zade is a tower of strength.'

'What about Stella?' Catrina blurted out, instantly wishing the question back.

'Don't let her bother you.' Jean tucked Catrina's hand under her own arm and looked at her seriously. 'She's always been after Zade. He chose you. She'll settle to the idea.'

Catrina didn't think so, but she kept her speculations to herself and went with Zade's mother to meet everyone—neighbours who greeted her warmly and the ranch hands who treated her with a great deal of respect and called her ma'am.

'Well, I'm not going to be lonely,' Catrina laughed, looking at Zade's mother. 'I don't think I've seen so many people gathered in one room before.'

'It's big enough to hold them,' Jean Mackensie said, looking round at the huge living-room of the ranch house. 'You'll see its size when they've all finally gone. This is just a social gathering, Catrina. We have them from time to time, but mostly it's quiet, still and calm. I like it like that. When the neighbours have gone and the boys have got their orders for morning and gone back to their quarters, you'll really be able to look at the place, because there'll only be the two of you.'

'Don't you live with Zade?' Catrina looked startled. She had gained the impression that they lived together, still in the ranch house as a family, although Zade had never said so.

'We don't! Let Bart loose here and he never knows when to stop. He's retired, taking it easy. We live a few miles away, still on Mackensie land, but just far enough away to keep Bart from getting into things. His heart's a bit dodgy, but don't let him know I told you. We're supposed to ignore it. He does.'

'Isn't it a little dangerous to be so far from civilisation, then?'

Catrina's question brought a gurgling laugh to Jean's lips.

'Don't let anyone hear you say that, love. As far as Zade and the rest are concerned this *is* civilisation and nothing else matches it. As to Bart, he's all right. If any help is needed it's here fast and Zade has the helicopter anyway. Bart's no invalid. It's just a heart murmur.'

Catrina decided to let the matter drop. The thought of illness made her realise how isolated they seemed to be here and it brought back the knowledge that if Zade should ignore her she had nothing to look forward to but unhappiness.

She was reminded of that when they had all gone at last and the room was empty and huge, the fire dying in the great fireplace.

'I'd better clear up,' she said into the silence as Zade stood musing over some of the papers that Bart had been discussing with him earlier.

'Leave it. Morning's soon enough.' He never even took his eyes from the papers and Catrina's spirits sank a little lower before annoyance set in. It would be a great life if he simply intended to aim words at her in that disinterested manner.

'I prefer to start now,' she snapped. 'At least I can get things into the kitchen.' She had been greatly relieved to find a modern, gleaming kitchen as Jean had given her a brief tour of the lower rooms of the ranch house, but she hadn't noticed a dishwasher. She wasn't used to dealing with people in vast numbers and her eyes had taken in the plates and glasses that were strewn around the room. Far from not knowing what her duties were as Zade's wife, it looked as if she would be tossed in at the deep end. Catrina hadn't forgotten that Zade was an early riser and, in any case, she had heard him talking to the men about a five-thirty gathering. They simply took it for granted. She wondered how many would want breakfast at this alarmingly early hour. Did they feed themselves or would she be doing it?

When she glanced up angrily, Zade was regarding her with amused interest, noting the mutinous set of her mouth.

'Getting ready to be elbow-deep in washing up at four in the morning?' he enquired drily. 'These things will be done while you're still enjoying your beauty sleep. Hank will have this lot cleared, washed and away while you're dreaming about it.'

'Who's Hank?' Catrina looked at him with irritated suspicion and he walked over to a huge, old desk, slipping the papers into a drawer and slanting her another amused look.

'Hank Torrance just about runs the house.'

'You've got a manservant?' Catrina stared at him in amazement and he suddenly grinned to himself.

'Please don't mention it. He'd have my hide and he certainly doesn't look the part. Hank used to be the camp cook when Bart still ran a chuck wagon. That was a long time ago. The outfit's too big now, too complicated, so Hank just moved across to the house. He's close on seventy, vindictive as a weasel, and boss of the kitchen. Keep out from under his feet. He irritates fast. As to the house, a couple of the boys are married. Their wives clean here. So far, twice a week has been enough for me, but you may want them more often, just let them know. No problem.'

Catrina felt temper fade into dismay. A vicious old cook, an indifferent husband and two unknown women who would clean the ranch house as usual. At that moment the Mackensie ranch seemed more lonely than ever and far away from anything that could even loosely be called civilisation.

'What am I supposed to do?' she asked quietly, looking away from the derision that now gleamed in Zade's eyes.

'Not a lot. You're the boss's wife. You'll get the hang of it.' He suddenly seemed to tire of the quietly goading tone and turned abruptly away. 'After you've settled in you'll probably want to change a few things. Please yourself. Money's no object. Just leave this area alone, though,' he added, indicating the desk and the im-mediate surroundings. 'I have no study and don't plan to use one in the future. I like working in here. Anything else you can change. It doesn't matter to me.' He walked to the door, clearly expecting her to follow. 'I'll get our things upstairs. Plenty of time to unpack tomorrow. You look ready to drop.'

She was, for more reasons than one. Long hours of travel had left her jaded and the welcoming party had been quite a strain. Now, though, things were worse. She had never imagined she would be here, so far away from anyone, with time hanging on her hands. Zade would work all day and work at that great, old desk each evening. She knew already how things would be. He would ignore her.

Catrina walked upstairs behind him, watching the effortless way he handled their luggage. He did everything like that and right at this moment she felt utterly inadequate. He shouldered a door open off the long, wide passage and she brightened a little. At least she was his wife. He needed her.

'I'll drop your things off here for now,' Zade said, putting her cases by a huge bed. 'You might want to move when you've had the chance to look around, but, for now, this bed is made up and you're tired. Leave everything until morning. If you want anything, I'm next door, but don't be long deciding. I'll be out like a light as my head touches the pillow.'

Catrina stood by the bed and stared at him in dismay.

'You...you mean we have separate rooms,' she managed chokily.

'I'll be up at five,' he pointed out in a patient voice. The boys will be round at five-thirty and we'll be away. No sense in disturbing you.'

'We...we're supposed to be married... I mean...what will they think?'

'The boys? I don't plan to mention it to them.' Zade looked at her as if she were slightly mad. He was instantly back to quiet goading and Catrina's face flushed with embarrassment.

'I was talking about the women who clean the house. Do you want it all over the district that...that...'

'That I don't sleep with my wife?' His lips twisted wryly, his eyes glinting at her, brilliantly blue and touched with derision. 'If it bothers you then clean up here yourself.' He walked out while she was still staring at him in disbelief and for a long time she stared at the closed door. She wasn't really anything at all. She might be Zade's wife, but she had been wrong about one thing. He didn't need her. Why had he made love to her for one whole blissful night? Why had he married her?

A face came into her mind, a tanned face with green eyes that had watched her resentfully. It had always been clear that Zade was a law unto himself; she had realised that the moment she had seen him. Was the only reason for this marriage a stage in some battle she knew nothing of? She didn't know Zade at all. She had not even begun to get to know him. She probably never would. Catrina got ready for bed and inside she had an empty feeling that was growing deeper and wider with every passing minute.

CHAPTER EIGHT

THE house was silent when Catrina awoke next day. The room was comfortably warm, something she had been too dazed to notice the night before. There were radiators and clearly there was some form of central heating even though they were way out here. She remembered the huge cylindrical tanks she had seen behind the house; she had noticed their size the night before as they had arrived. Gas. Of course. That was how the kitchen ran too, no doubt.

She realised she was thinking about such practical problems to take her mind off more pressing matters and she pulled herself up sharply. It was no use lingering here. Things had to be faced and they could not be faced by hiding.

It was sunny, looking crisp and cold outside, and from the window she could see miles of open country, rolling plains and softly rounded hills. Her room was at the front of the house. It was Zade who had the view of the mountains. Once again she stifled her thoughts as she began to wonder how long Zade would want her here if she was not pregnant after all. She felt used, bewildered, and always the face with the green eyes floated into her head.

There wasn't a soul in sight. It was seven and by now Zade and the men would be a long way from the ranch house. She went to shower, discovering a modern bathroom down the passage, and then she prepared to face the day, Hank's uncertain temper and anything else that was necessary. She had brought this all on herself by falling in love with Zade and even if he felt nothing the magic was too strong for her to contemplate asking to leave, now or ever.

Nobody seemed to be around when she got down the stairs. A quick look into the huge living-room showed her that last night's signs of revelry had been cleared. So Hank was on the job, even though he was not immediately visible. She wandered into the warm kitchen that was filled with the smell of breakfast and it reminded her that she was hungry. She had been too tight inside to eat last night.

'Ready for breakfast, Miz Mackensie?'

Catrina jumped at the sound of the voice. It had the croaking depth of a bullfrog and she spun round to face the man who had come so silently into the kitchen.

Zade had warned her, but she was quite unprepared to meet Hank Torrance, and for a second she just stared. He was almost completely bald, although his bushy white eyebrows would have won a prize. A very tall, stringy old man, with a slight stoop and a hot-tempered look in his eyes, he seemed to be almost anything but a cook.

He was wearing an open-necked, checked shirt, a spotlessly clean white undershirt showing beneath it. The white apron tied haphazardly round his waist was clean too, covering black trousers and almost reaching the top of riding boots. He was watching her steadily, assessing her, and she realised that, whatever his age, this man was nobody's fool. He looked alarmingly in charge.

'Er—thank you. I'm hungry.' Catrina didn't know exactly how to react to him. It would have been more normal to be running around after a man of this age, telling him to sit down and getting a meal for him. The men of this age who came to the library had often needed a good deal of help. She could see, though, that any offer of help would receive some crisply hot comment from Hank. This was his kitchen and she knew she would not be allowed to forget it.

'Soon see to that,' he muttered, moving over to the cooker. 'Been expecting you. Things are well nigh ready. There's bacon and eggs, hot cakes 'n' syrup, and biscuits with honey. You can have coffee or tea. I know all about tea. When Bart ran things, Miz Mackensie liked her tea, bein' English like you.'

'Er—I don't usually eat a lot at breakfast,' Catrina began, stunned at the list of food.

'Don't expect you to eat like a ranch hand at round-up,' he grunted. 'I cut it down to suit your size. Leave anything you don't want,' he added. His back was to Catrina as he worked at the cooker, but his final remark sounded a bit threatening, and she was still looking at him warily as he turned with her plate piled up with food and walked across to put it on the table in front of her. 'You can eat here if you've a mind to,' he offered, and Catrina saw just a faint trace of a smile round the tight mouth. 'You're a slip of a thing all right. I'll watch you get round that.'

He nodded to the food on her plate and to her surprise he poured himself a mug of steaming coffee and pulled up a chair at the other side of the table. It was a good thing she felt hungry. Hank Torrance was going to supervise her appetite.

'Don't often invite folks to eat in my kitchen,' he remarked, his eyes taking in her appearance. 'Missed out on you last night, though. Don't like social events. This gives me a chance to look you over.'

Catrina just gazed at him in amazement. He certainly believed in straight talking. The old eyes looked as keen as those of any younger man, crinkled with years of looking into the sun and wind. His face was weather-beaten, deeply lined, but he was sharp as a needle and quite obviously missed nothing at all. She hastily got on with her meal. He was summing her up and a smile was growing at the back of the pale blue eyes.

'The boss is a tough man,' he commented after inspecting her. 'Hard. Works like the boys. There's nothin' they can do that he can't. On top of that, he flies that helicopter and manages the ranch. He's a businessman too. I reckon he can just about do anything. Known him since he was nothin' more than a boy.'

'Is...is this a big place to run?' Catrina ventured, astonished that this rather forbidding old man was determined to talk to her.

'Seventy thousand acres. Last count we had six thousand head of cattle. There'll be more come spring round-up. You'll hardly see the boss then when the crews are drivin' the cattle in from the winter ranges. It's workin', ridin' and brandin' all day for about four to five weeks 'til they're all on the summer grazing.'

'Did Mrs Mackensie go with them, when she was here?' Catrina asked hopefully, wondering what she would do with her time even now, let alone when Zade disappeared for days on end.

'No, ma'am. No place for a woman. Even Miss Cunningham don't try it an' she's ranching stock, born and bred.'

It rang dismally of Mrs Hudson, 'farm born and bred', and Catrina hastily changed the subject.

'Do you live in the house—er—Mr Torrance?'

'Call me Hank. Get to feeling old with this "Mr" business. No, I don't live in the house. Got my own quarters, same as I had when I was out on the range myself. Drove the old chuck wagon then, but it's gone, like most things. It's easier in the kitchen now I've got the hang of the cooker. Sure miss the old wood stove, though. Could turn out breakfast for twelve men at four in the morning at round-up times. Could cook a mean set of pies for dinner. No trouble.' He pushed out his bottom lip reminiscently and then shrugged his shoulders. 'Times change. You'll see.'

Catrina could already see. Times had changed for her very quickly. They would change even more.

'Reckon you'll cope,' Hank volunteered unexpectedly. 'Got a look to you.' He stood and looked down at her, a wry smile touching his lips. 'See you got tucked into that, anyways. See what we can do with you at lunchtime.' She could see what he meant. Her plate was cleared, not a scrap of food left, and there was a cunning glow to the old eyes that now regarded her with amusement.

'I don't normally eat so much,' Catrina warned him firmly.

'Good cooking tells,' he said without any sign of boasting. 'Could see you were nervous, first day and all. That's why I sat and talked. Don't usually bother.'

He walked off and Catrina found a smile growing across her face as she watched him leave. The back of his neck was a bit red. Whatever his excuse, he had wanted to have a chat with her. She might just have an ally there—if she watched her step.

It reminded her that pretty soon the women who cleaned would be coming, always assuming that this was their day. Before then she had to make the bed up in her room as if nobody had slept there. She also had to hide her things. It might not bother Zade that people knew they had separate rooms, but it bothered her very much indeed. As soon as Hank was out of sight, she shot off up the stairs and dived into her room.

There was a good deal of chaos. Last night she had been very tired and now she looked round dismally deciding to put her clothes away first. She couldn't even afford to leave anything on the dressing-table, no clues that this room was in use at all. It made her thoroughly miserable. At this rate she would always be a stranger in this house with no small nook or cranny to call her own. And it was one thing for Zade to tell her to change anything she wished. It would be another to do it. She rather suspected that he wouldn't welcome change any more than Hank did. It looked as if she was still an 'outsider'.

Unpacking took a good deal longer than she had expected. All the time she was listening for the sound of the women arriving. She wished crossly that she had asked Hank, but then he would have perhaps found it surprising that her own husband hadn't told her. The whole situation was ridiculously complicated and Catrina's temper began to grow with every passing minute. She wasn't used to creeping about like a convict.

'Anybody home?'

The unexpectedly close call had Catrina looking round the room frantically. Somebody was here after all, actually upstairs, and she hadn't even got all her clothes away yet. The bed was unmade—a complete give-away. Her face flushed with confusion and she was standing almost at bay when Stella Cunningham walked into the room.

'Oh, you're here? Not a soul downstairs.' She regarded Catrina with amused eyes and leaned against the doorway. Once again she was in jeans and a checked shirt, but, all the same, she managed to make Catrina feel untidy and flustered. For the first time Catrina noticed her hair. It was a sort of dark blonde, long and tied back, emphasising the green-eyed, tanned face.

'Zade is out,' she said uncomfortably. She had no desire to chat to this woman and she felt as if she had been cornered quite deliberately.

'I know. He took the helicopter out this morning. He's going round the whole ranch to look things over. I expect he'll call at our place for lunch. He normally does.'

'Are you far away?' Catrina asked, still clearing her clothes away and stifling her miserable burst of jealousy that Stella knew exactly where Zade was when she didn't even know herself.

'Our place is closer to town. We're not too far off, as a matter of fact, because our house is at the edge of the spread. It's more convenient.'

More convenient for what? Meeting Zade?

'You're sleeping in the guest room? What's this, an English habit?' Stella's face was filled with malicious amusement and Catrina turned on her sharply.

'I was tired last night. Zade had to be up early and he wanted me to sleep in. I've only just had breakfast.'

'Why waste your time putting clothes into this wardrobe, then?' There was absolutely no subtlety in Stella's question and Catrina felt her cheeks grow hotter than ever.

'Too many clothes for the other wardrobe,' she managed, but it did not have the desired effect.

'Zade's got plenty of wardrobe space. Maybe you should fill that up first, leave summer clothes in here— unless you plan to stay in separate rooms?'

'We do not!' Catrina said heatedly. 'I'm just trying to get some order into things before the women come to clean.'

'Millie and Liz come this afternoon. Mondays and Fridays.'

'You seem to know how things work,' Catrina said, making herself face the taunting eyes.

'I know every inch of the place. I've been coming here since Zade was a child.'

'He was a teenager when he first came here,' Catrina pointed out triumphantly. 'I doubt if he ever was a child,' she added crossly, angered beyond belief with Zade for letting her in for this.

'He's hard with some people,' Stella agreed. 'I know him, though. I imagine you're going to be pretty bored here. For a lot of the time we almost live on horseback.'

'I can ride,' Catrina said flatly. 'There'll be plenty to do when I've got the hang of things.'

'You ride?' The green eyes narrowed with annoyance for one second and then there was a definite curl to Stella's lips. 'Oh, English riding. I've seen it on films—hacking. You'll not last long in the saddle here. Well, I'll be off. I want to be back before lunch.'

She disappeared as swiftly as she had come and Catrina sat on the bed, raging inside. If Zade thought he was getting away with this he could think again. It was quite clear now that Stella knew exactly where Zade's room was. She even knew how much wardrobe space he had. Catrina got to her feet and stormed off out into the passage, opening doors and slamming them closed until she found Zade's room.

It was just as she had thought. He *did* have a wonderful view of the mountains. He had a private bathroom too and enough wardrobe space to make any two models feel secure. It was a lovely room. With a bit of alteration it could be made perfect. She went out and slammed the door enough to make the house shake. She was not going to sit miserably in Zade's room, dreaming about him and feeling close to tears. If she had to have the other room she would set it up nicely and anyone who discovered the terrible secret of husband and wife being separated could just go and tell everyone else in Montana!

Catrina's temper did not die all day, even though two middle-aged women arrived after lunch and cleaned the house, talking comfortably and non-stop all the time. She could see that she would get on with them easily. Millie Dawson and Liz Brennan were wives of two of the hands and by the time they left she knew as much about the place and the people as she could take in at one go.

At lunchtime, Hank appeared and invited her to eat in his kitchen as she was still 'lonesome'. It pleased her greatly that she was sliding into the affections of the old man. She had the feeling, gained from one or two pithy comments, that she was one up on Miss Cunningham. It did not, however, make her any more pleased about the state of affairs, and she was still quietly boiling when Zade came back.

It was almost dark. She was in her room, putting the finishing touches to her arrangements, when the station wagon drew up at the front of the house. As she looked down, Zade got out and slammed the door. He looked tired, but she had not one bit of sympathy for him. The lean, tanned face was set grimly and she stifled the flood of feeling that came as she saw him. He must have had a long lunch break at Stella's place if he was only just arriving back now. She deliberately stayed where she was. If he wanted to greet her, he could find her.

He did not come to find her. Finally she could not hold the temper in and stay in her room. She got ready and went downstairs. Hank had made the fire up early on and as she walked into the lamp-lit living room Zade was working at his desk.

He put his pen down as she came in and just stared at her thoughtfully. There was little doubt that he could see angry discontent on her face, but he ignored it. The brilliant eyes moved over her as she stood in the doorway. She was wearing a red woollen dress, bright and vivid against her black shining curls, and she had the feeling that her cheeks were an exact matching red, partially from temper and partially from the yearning that shot through her as Zade inspected her minutely.

'Had a good day?' he enquired slowly, his eyes narrowed on her rather mutinous face.

'Interesting,' Catrina said shortly.

'How's that?' He leaned back and hooked his leg over the arm of the chair, quite obviously prepared to listen to her silly chatter about her pointless day. It infuriated her more, but she kept her rage well under control.

'I met the ladies, of course—Millie and Liz. I got on with them splendidly. They'll come in more often if I want them, but that can wait a while.'

'Fine. I expect you met Hank?' Zade's lips twitched in amusement and Catrina looked at him with bright-eyed triumph.

'Yes. I had breakfast with him in the kitchen, of course. He had it all ready for me.'

'You'd better forget the "of course" bit,' Zade warned seriously. 'Hank keeps his kitchen off limits. He's probably feeling too irritated to make dinner now.'

'We discussed dinner,' Catrina told him loftily. 'As to breakfast, he invited me to stay in the kitchen. He had coffee and sat talking. It was most interesting, all about the old days. He must have enjoyed it too because he served my lunch there and ate with me. He seemed to think it was dismal in the dining-room and I must say I agree with him.'

'I'll be damned!' Zade murmured, his blue eyes wide open in amazement, and Catrina thought sourly that he probably would be. 'Nobody gets round Hank,' he added.

'I never tried,' Catrina said starchily. 'We just seemed to get on well, that's all.'

Hank popped his head round the door at that moment and looked grimly at Zade.

'Twenty minutes,' he said curtly. 'If you want to change, better hop to it.'

He went out, looking as sour as Catrina felt, and she didn't know if something had ruffled his feathers or if he was just back to normal. Zade seemed to take it all in his stride because he stood and made for the door with nothing more than a deeply considering look at Catrina.

They ate in the dubious splendour of the dining-room. Zade appeared just before Hank served the meal. He had showered and changed and now he was in dark trousers and wearing a blue checked shirt. It picked up the colour of his eyes, eyes that fixed on Catrina the moment he came into the room. He looked so wonderful that it made her head spin, but it was not at all difficult to keep her emotions in order. Somehow or other the checked shirt reminded her of Stella and it was enough to keep her face set in the lines of temper that had been there all afternoon.

They hardly spoke during the meal. Hank served each course with a grimly set face as if he was expecting harsh comments. Everything was delicious and Catrina ate as much as she could, not wanting to offend him. In the meantime, her eyes roamed round the room. It was awful. The furniture was very good and well cared for, rather stately, in the old American style, but the walls were covered in paper that almost gave her a headache and the curtains were dismal, depressing. This room would have to go!

'Coffee in the other room, Miz Mackensie?' Hank came in to enquire, ignoring Zade, and looking with satisfaction at her almost cleaned plate.

'Thank you, Hank. This is no place to linger.'

'Sure enough right,' he agreed.

'That meal was wonderful,' Catrina praised, really meaning it.

'Good cooking tells,' he pointed out again, nodding at her with grim satisfaction. 'I'll bring the coffee things.'

Zade said nothing, but she could almost feel his laughter as he walked behind her to the living-room and the blazing fire. It looked as if he was going to sit with his coffee, stare at her, and make no comments at all. Catrina wasn't allowing it.

'If you meant what you said about changing things——' she began, throwing her head back proudly.

'I did,' he interrupted. 'I take it that the dining-room is about to be savaged? Please yourself, but don't get too enthusiastic about ordering furniture yet. We don't know that the snow has finished. Could be a heavy fall any time to May. It would make furniture-moving tricky.'

'There's nothing wrong with the furniture,' Catrina said sharply, irritated that he seemed to think she would throw everything out and bring in modern things that would not at all fit into the atmosphere of the old ranch house. 'It's the curtains, the walls. I refuse to live with faded blue roses and tarnished gold stripes.'

'That paper was there when Bart's mother lived in the ranch house,' Zade informed her, his lips quirking at her attitude. 'It's a museum item.'

'Then the museum can collect it if they're interested,' Catrina said tartly. 'I'm surprised your mother didn't want to see the back of it.'

'She did. Bart refused to see it go. Dug his heels in.'

'Oh!' Catrina's bad-tempered enthusiasm waned a little. 'Will he mind if I get rid of it?'

'The ranch is mine,' Zade stated shortly, 'lock, stock and barrel. Bart just keeps enough shares to give him the right to interfere when the mood's on him. You change what you want. You're talking to the boss right now. I should think my mother will be delighted. She'll probably be over here tearing it off the wall when she hears.'

'Good. Then I'll plan it and you can tell me where to order things from, or maybe your mother will tell me if you're too busy to take any interest.'

Zade was lying back in an armchair, his leg hooked over the arm again, and Catrina sat primly on the very front edge of the facing settee. She had said all she intended to say and now her lips were set in one tight line. She wasn't used to being awkward and unpleasant, but she could be if she tried.

There was the fire crackling, the wind whining in the chimney, and not another sound. She deliberately didn't look at Zade, but she was so much on edge that when Hank went and the back door banged in the wind she jumped visibly. Zade turned lazily towards her.

'OK! Let's have it. What's eating you?'

'Nothing!'

'You normally look all uptight and mean as a polecat?' He regarded her quizzically and she glared at him, her cheeks flushing with temper.

'I don't believe so. I don't normally have neighbours invading my privacy either, walking uninvited into my house and then into my bedroom and commenting on the use of separate sleeping arrangements!'

She got the full benefit of Zade's brilliantly blue eyes then, his undivided attention.

'Come again?' he ordered softly.

'Oh, I think you understand,' Catrina snapped, everything pouring out in a rage. 'Stella Cunningham obviously knows her way around the house, is obviously used to just walking in unannounced and clearly capable of finding her way around upstairs. She came this morning when I was putting my clothes away and walked in with very keen interest. The bed is quite big enough for two, but she never faltered. It was not your room and she knew that very well. She drew her own conclusions—audibly!'

The blue eyes were now narrowed and flashing off sparks that threatened to set her ablaze, but Zade said nothing at all. He simply stood and walked out of the room, leaving her sitting there, her temper dying and sheer misery taking its place. He hadn't denied a single thing. He hadn't explained anything either. It was perfectly clear that Stella had been here more than once with Zade. It was just as she had suspected—she was in a bitter game she knew nothing about.

He was about ten minutes and then he walked in, grabbed her wrist, and marched her out, switching off the lights as he went.

'What are you doing?' Catrina struggled furiously, hurting very badly inside and not at all sure of Zade's intentions. 'I'm not ready for bed and I'm not going.'

'You're going, Catrina,' he assured her tersely. 'I've got to be up early again and when I go you go.'

If he thought he was sending her to bed like an unruly child he was mistaken and Catrina began to struggle even more. It didn't bother him unduly. He simply picked her up and continued, ignoring the way she pushed against his shoulder and kicked out her legs. He didn't put her down until he had walked right into his room and then he let her feet touch the floor, but he still kept a tightly restraining hand on her arm.

'Your things, Miz Mackensie!' he snapped, turning her to the still-open doors of the wardrobe where at least half her clothes were ranged alongside his. Her make-up was on the dressing-table too and now she felt just a bit scared. 'You can rearrange everything tomorrow,' he added tightly, 'but for now you're more or less moved, so get ready for bed.'

'I won't!' Catrina blushed to the roots of her hair and tried again to get away, but it was clearly only what he had expected. One iron-strong arm lashed round her and she was securely trapped as he turned her away and the zip of her dress plunged down.

She began to tremble, tears coming to the back of her eyes. Before when Zade had made love to her it had been magical, but this was harsh, cold-blooded, frightening.

'Please, Zade!' All the fight had gone out of her and he turned her to face him, sliding her dress away, his eyes running over her as she stood in a lacy slip, her head hanging down in embarrassment and misery.

'You don't want to sleep with me after all?' he taunted, and it was enough to have the tears escaping on to her soft cheeks, clearly visible as he tilted her face with one strong brown hand. He looked at her for a second and then folded her into his arms, drawing her against his warmth. 'Come on, honey,' he said softly. 'It's bedtime.'

She just stopped struggling, stopped crying, and Zade cupped her face in his hands, wiping her tears away and then covering her mouth with his in a kiss so gentle that she might have been a worn-out child who needed comfort. Responding to him was as natural as breathing and as her arms wound round his neck his hands slid to her shoulders and then lower as he slowly finished undressing her. Catrina had never noticed that he had put the nightie she had left out on the bed until it slid over her head and he released her to pull her arms through the sleeves.

She was in a daze as he lifted her into bed and stared at him wildly as he started to put out the lights. What was he going to do, walk off and leave her here while he now slept in the other room?

'I'm going to bank down the fire,' he explained quietly, seeing her panic. 'Can't think what Hank would say if I let the house burn down.'

By the time he came back up, Catrina was dreamy, almost asleep, unable to understand what was happening. It didn't alter anything, though. There was still Stella. He had been with Stella a long time even today. It had been Catrina's first day in a strange place, but he hadn't bothered about that. She turned over on her side, her back to where Zade would be, and tears came to her eyes again because she had forgotten in her temper just what it was like when he held her and kissed her. She felt worse than ever, really. It would have been better to go to her own bed and seethe with rage all night.

When he came up, Catrina pretended to be asleep, but Zade wasn't fooled at all. He got into bed and then switched on the lamp, turning her round and seeing the tears lingering on her thick, dark lashes.

'Do you hate it here?' he asked seriously when she just lay still and looked at him. She simply shook her head.

'I could be happy here. I know it, but——'

'But what?' He slid his arms around her, drawing her close, and she looked up into his eyes, dazzled as ever, bewitched as ever.

'You were out all day.' Her eyes were accusing, but he seemed to deliberately misunderstand.

'You're not a baby. You seem to have had a whole lot of company.' And some of it she could have done without! Catrina's eyes flashed and she tried to pull away, but he simply tightened his arm, the other hand capturing her face. 'I had to take stock. I've been away a long time and this is a big place to supervise,' he insisted.

'But you took a long lunch break with Stella!' Catrina snapped, instantly ashamed and embarrassed. He gave her one of his deep, long looks, but he didn't let her go.

'I had cheese, bread and hot coffee,' he assured her, 'and not a lot of that.'

'Is she too mean to feed you?' Catrina raged, seeing now that it was all true.

'She never gets the chance,' he informed her softly, his eyes locked with hers. 'I ate at one of the line shacks with a couple of the boys. Tomorrow I'll have to fly out there and top up their rations. They've another week to go before the relief team gets up to them.'

'Stella said——'

'Stella likes trouble,' he said softly, still looking at her. 'She sure made plenty for me tonight.' He smiled slowly, his eyes moving over her face. 'So I've got a jealous wife with a tongue to match Hank's. No wonder he thinks highly of you; you're a girl after his own heart.'

'I'm not jealous,' Catrina protested shakily, but he just smiled at her derisively and reached back to put out the light.

'Then I can rest easy. Goodnight, Catrina.'

She tried to move away when it was clear that he wasn't a bit interested in her now that he had things settled and back in order. His arms tightened round her and he pulled her head to his shoulder, moving until she was comfortable.

'Go to sleep,' he murmured. 'I'm up at five.'

Catrina went as still as a mouse, warmth flooding through her. For a second he stroked her hair and then he was asleep, leaving her trembling and puzzled. At least she was with him and he hadn't been to see Stella. She never doubted his word. If Zade had been there he would have said so and not bothered at all what she thought. She snuggled her head against him, going still again when he seemed to stiffen. He had to be up early. It wouldn't do to wake him by moving about.

CHAPTER NINE

ZADE was awake before it was quite light next morning and as he stirred Catrina awoke too. She was lying in his arms as she had been the night before and it must have been his attempts to extricate himself that woke her.

'Go back to sleep,' he advised. 'There's no need whatever for you to be up at this hour.'

'What are you going to do today?' It was enchanting to be lying in his arms; Catrina looked up at him, her soft brown eyes glowing, and he seemed to be quite content to stay where he was for the moment and look back at her.

'Up to the line camp to take some stores. The boys have been eating me out of house and home.'

'Are you going straight after breakfast?' She felt a little nervous about her decision to be bold with Zade, but she already knew what she was going to ask.

'Yes. Any comments?' He looked at her in amusement and she took advantage of the softened moment.

'Can I come with you?'

Her request seemed to startle Zade. For a moment he looked into her eager face and said nothing and Catrina felt the eagerness fading away.

'If you don't want me to come...'

'I'm making rapid calculations,' he explained with patient humour. 'I'm weighing up what I've got to carry and how much difference you'll make. A captain has to trim his vessel. Still, you'll not make much difference. There's not a lot of you, though if Hank keeps feeding

150

you up we'll have to have you weighed with the stores before any future trips.'

'Oh, thank you!' Catrina gazed at him with shining eyes and he grinned down at her before moving away and reaching for his clothes. She didn't take her eyes off him. She just couldn't. She had never seen Zade dress before and it reminded her that he was her husband. She was still watching him when he turned, tucking a thick shirt into his jeans and looking at her in real amusement.

'Going to move?' he enquired wryly. 'I doubt Hank will ever get to the breakfast-in-bed bit.'

'I...I'll be two minutes,' she said shakily, still gazing at him with glowing eyes. 'Th-thank you for letting me come.'

'You're easy enough to please,' he commented drily, and she couldn't tell whether he meant about the trip or her unashamed watching of him. She flushed in confusion and he grinned at her, turning to the door and issuing orders as he went.

'Breakfast in two minutes. Get moving, Star-eyes.'

She had never moved so fast in her life. As she peeped from the door she saw Zade go into the other bathroom and she felt a small glow again. He had left this bathroom for her. Just little things from Zade made her feel pampered and she was going with him! She sang under her breath all the time and arrived downstairs just behind him, her face flushed and her smile sweetly happy.

There was a small commotion in the kitchen and she could see why the table there was so big. There were four men having breakfast and Hank turned from the cooker as she came in, his face falling.

'Can't have her to yourself today, Hank,' Zade remarked, pulling a chair out for Catrina and then hooking one forward for himself. As she had come in, the men had all stood and looked at her a little sheepishly. A couple of them hadn't shaved and now they looked as if they regretted it.

'Taking her up to the line shack?' Hank demanded fiercely, ignoring Zade's taunting words. 'It'll be mighty cold up there.'

'She knows.' Zade took the plate that Hank handed to him, wincing and putting it down fast before glaring at the old man. He was ignored and Catrina had a plate brought specially, a white cloth holding it.

'Watch this plate, Miz Mackensie. It's real hot.' She looked at Zade, her eyes dancing, and his lips twisted in amusement. Hank hadn't bothered to answer back when Zade had teased; he had his own methods of retaliation.

She was introduced to the men, who now seemed to have recovered from surprise. One of them was a young man straight from college who looked at Catrina in admiration.

'Herbie Moore,' Zade introduced. 'He's doing a stint on the ranch before taking up his new job.'

'I'll be here a year,' Herbie promised happily, his eyes on Catrina's beautiful colouring, her clear skin and shining curls. 'If the boss doesn't throw me out.'

'What job are you going to when you finally leave here?' Catrina asked. She wasn't a bit shy with these tough men. They were quiet and polite, beginning to relax in her presence.

'Dad's got an electronics firm. I'm going into that. I'll take over one day so there's no point in ducking out.'

'Doesn't he mind you taking time off to be here?' Catrina asked with interest. The men laughed and Herbie grinned at her.

'It was his idea, ma'am. He knows the boss well. He thinks college is a soft option. This is to get me on my toes and as to time off—what's that?' He looked wryly at Zade, who was already consulting his watch.

'Five-thirty,' he announced, pushing his own plate away. 'Hop to it.' They all went out grinning, nodding happily at Catrina, and she pushed her plate away too, her food only half finished, much to Hank's frowning annoyance.

'You want a hot-water bottle for in that helicopter, Miz Mackensie?' he asked ferociously, and Zade frowned at him with equal ferocity.

'Listen, you misery, I'm toughening her up, not softening her up. She'll be brought back in one piece and you can throw a blanket over her then.'

'Don't care one way or the other,' Hank snapped, and Zade took Catrina firmly by the arm, leading her out of the warm kitchen.

'That's easy to see,' he remarked drily. He stood waiting for her as she put on one of her warm coats, muttering in exasperation when he looked up to see Hank at the kitchen door wiping his hands on the white cloth and supervising things from a distance.

'I'm going to have trouble with that old fool,' he said as he helped Catrina into the station wagon. 'He's one hell of a nursemaid. You must bring out the mothering instinct in him. Any other female arriving when he was serving the boys would have brought on a crisis. All he did was burn my hand for being sassy.'

Catrina said nothing. She was snuggling into her hood, smiling to herself. So far, her day was very successful, very successful indeed.

Excitement rose again as they came to the helicopter, parked in a shed not too far from the house, but just a little too far to have walked to it. A couple of the men were already there, bringing it out, and soon she was safely inside as Zade checked around and the men loaded the stores.

She watched them leave. They were on horseback. Her first real glimpse of cowboys. She watched the way they rode, almost part of the horse. It reminded her of Stella's words and she turned back to find Zade beside her, watching her curiously.

'Can I ride with you—when you go out, I mean?' she asked before he could speak.

'Sure,' he promised slowly. 'Let's do one thing at a time, though, shall we? At the moment we're flying, or we will be when we stop nattering on.'

'I'm sorry,' Catrina said seriously. 'I can wait, of course, but I want to ride like that as soon as possible.' She pointed to the men, who were now a good distance away. 'Stella seems to think that I hack.'

Zade threw his head back and laughed, slanting her a blue-eyed look that quite shook her.

'Oh, we'll get you going in no time,' he assured her in amusement. 'I can't have you hacking. It would be bad for my image.' He was still grinning as he reached back and claimed his hat, sticking it on his head at a rakish angle. It was a white stetson with a curled brim and it looked wonderful, but Catrina giggled.

'So what now?' He smiled across at her and she looked at him with dancing eyes.

'You look like a cowboy.'

'Well, I try, I really do,' he assured her, and then his long fingers were at the controls and the machine sprang into life, noisily and easily, and Catrina wasn't even slightly worried as they lifted off from the snowy ground. Hank was quite right. Zade could do anything. She hugged herself with joy because today things were ever so slightly different. Zade had let her into his life and she would just keep on going, one step at a time.

'Scared?' Zade glanced across at her and she shook her head, smiling at him.

'Not a bit. It's wonderful. Are we going into the mountains?'

'No. Just to the edge. Too far to take either the car or the pick-up, and some deep snow on the way. The boys take it in turns up here because the cattle need winter feed. There are new calves too. It's hard. I work two teams up away from the ranch house. They do three weeks each and that's more than enough.'

'Do they get snowed in?' Catrina asked in awe.

'They do. Strictly speaking, they're snowed in now. I'll have to bring them out when they come. I take in the other team at the same time.'

'Gosh!' Catrina murmured, very impressed, and when she looked up his mouth was curved in a softened smile.

'You sure are easy to please, Miz Mackensie,' he said quietly.

Catrina looked away, happiness washing over her. He had said that before and then he called her Star-eyes. Her eyes were starry now. He might not love her, but she knew now he would never be unkind to her, and she loved him more every day.

It was the beginning of a very new time because Zade's subtly changed attitude made a great deal of difference. It wasn't lonely any more because he seemed to be around much more than she had expected and, although he spent a long time working either out of doors or at his desk, the brilliantly blue eyes smiled more often than not.

Jean and Bart Mackensie often dropped in and there was no sign at all of Stella. Gradually, Catrina got to know the men who worked around the ranch, and in a very short time England seemed far away.

The sleeping arrangements continued. She was there every night, sleeping beside Zade, but he never did more than hold her close, and that not very often. She dared not bring the subject up and as the days passed it became more and more frustrating to try to sleep when she wanted Zade's kisses so badly. He seemed to be quite indifferent.

It was frustration that finally drove her to drastic action as far as the dining-room was concerned. One morning she got up to find a warmer wind blowing, the snow almost gone. Looking out of the window, she could see it still lying deep on the distant hills, but around the ranch and across the rolling prairie it was melted, green grass showing through and spring at last in the air.

The distance was hazy blue, the far-off gullies shadowed with purple. Life was coming back to the land with soft colours and the low mountain ranges glittered white and crisp in the sun. It gave her energy and determination.

When she went down to breakfast, Zade had already left, and she wandered around restlessly before making a definite decision. She stood in the forbidding dining-room, frowning at the ghastly walls, and then marched to the kitchen and took out a bucket and an old knife. The sooner she got started the better. Hank was not around at the moment and there was no one at all to restrain her. If that paper was off, something would have to take its place.

Zade's mother arrived just before lunch and tracked Catrina down. Her face lit up when she found her new daughter-in-law vigorously scraping the walls, her black hair tied in a scarf and water splashing all over the wooden floor.

'At last it's going!' Jean exclaimed. 'Hallelujah! I've hated this for years.'

'Bart might not think this is a good idea,' Catrina pointed out, pausing for a moment. 'Wasn't it his mother's?'

'And her mother's before her, I should think,' Jean snorted. 'Hang on, I'll get a scraper of some sort.'

They were both busily working and talking when Stella arrived and it didn't take her long to find them. Clearly their activities stunned her because for a second she said nothing at all.

'Well? What do you think?' Jean asked, looking at her challengingly. Catrina had already discovered that Zade's mother was an irrepressible character and she was not disappointed now.

'Bart will fly off the handle,' Stella said smugly, but all she got was a scornful laugh.

'With Zade? That'll be the day! Anyway, this is Zade's place and has been for years. In Zade's place, Catrina can do exactly as she likes, and I've got that straight from the boss himself.'

'Anything I like except move his desk,' Catrina put in impishly, watching Stella's face redden with annoyance.

'Well, there's that,' Jean agreed with a laugh, and suddenly Catrina felt at home here, no longer threatened by Stella.

Hank walked in and after one look at Stella he made no comment at all about the activity.

'Lunch, Miz Mackensie,' he said curtly, but Catrina wasn't at all put out by his fierce looks now.

'Oh, can we have it in the kitchen, Hank?' she wheedled. She had hers there when she was alone, but if Zade was here they were dispatched to the dining-room, and Hank never volunteered to cope with more than one in his kitchen except for the early breakfast of the men. 'I know it's awkward when there's not just me, but——'

'Count me out,' Stella said crossly, turning to walk out of the house, and Hank's sour gaze followed her.

'Was going to, anyway,' he muttered. 'Ten minutes, then,' he added, looking at Catrina and Jean sternly.

'Fine.' She beamed at him and as he went Jean collapsed into silent laughter.

'You're making changes here, love,' she gurgled. 'I never did more than get Hank Torrance to make tea. He's taken you under his wing.'

'To Zade's vast irritation,' Catrina muttered. Suddenly she felt light-headed, a funny, feet-off-the-ground feeling, and she sat abruptly on the nearest chair.

'What is it?' Jean was beside her at once and Catrina gave her a rather wan smile.

'Nothing, really. I just felt a bit dizzy. It's probably because I'm hungry. You can get hungry without even knowing it. You get low blood-sugar.' Jean didn't look too impressed and neither did Hank, who was standing silently watching as she lifted her head.

'It's all this work,' was his uncalled-for comment, and Catrina pulled herself together sharply. She could see that this was about to be reported to Zade. The intention was clearly in Hank's eyes and she didn't want any interference.

All the same, she was a little silent at lunchtime, because she was doing some rapid calculations. It was true that she had missed her monthly enemy, but that was no unusual event. She had almost not noticed it. There was the change of life to this house, change of water, and the general upheaval. In any case, it was too early to be feeling faint, and she didn't want to think about any pregnancy. She was not close enough to Zade to be comfortable about it.

When Jean left in the early afternoon Catrina stubbornly continued, sneaking off as Hank went for his break and scraping away at the walls with an almost blank mind. It looked better without paper than it had done with that awful stuff, but she could see that it would need more than a coat of paint. She was standing back surveying it when Zade walked in silently.

His hands came down on her shoulders as she stood with her back to him and she jumped guiltily.

'Yes. You can jump,' he said severely, spinning her round to face him. 'According to your guardian angel you're working like a slave and fainting all over the place.'

'Oh, Zade!' Catrina said in exasperation. 'I didn't faint. I was a bit dizzy because I was hungry and, as to working like a slave, your mother helped gleefully. We did more talking than working.'

'It looks like it,' Zade muttered derisively, casting his eyes over the great area that had been stripped in such a short time. 'You can now stop. Upstairs and under the shower. Forget this. As it's so important to you I'll get Liz and Millie to do it.'

'You won't!' Catrina contradicted crossly, glaring up at him. 'I'll not be sent off like a child, and it's time Hank minded his own business.'

'I couldn't agree more,' Zade said, looking down at her annoyed face with a wry grin. 'Go and tell him. I'll just watch.'

'He'd probably leave,' Catrina murmured worriedly, her temper dying under the blaze of Zade's eyes.

'Leave you? He's more likely to cry.'

'Oh, Zade! Stop teasing,' she pleaded, and he smiled down at her, turning her to the door.

'If you leave it for today,' he promised. 'There's always tomorrow.'

'You don't take that attitude yourself. You never stop working.'

'I'm not a slender female with an exotic face,' Zade pointed out drily. 'As a matter of fact,' he added as she was slowly absorbing that, 'I was all set to take you to town. You can see if there's anything you want at the shops and we could stay out for dinner.'

Her face lit up and Zade looked down at her, shaking his head in amusement. She knew he was thinking yet again that she was easy to please, and with Zade she was. They were crossing the hall as Herbie came in, waving letters. It was his self-appointed task to get the mail and he delighted in bringing Catrina's. He was always excited about her letters from her father.

Her father wrote every week and had done since she was here. Sometimes his letters bore stamps from faraway places and Herbie was always interested.

'Two for you, boss,' he announced, 'and three for you, Mrs Mackensie. There's one from Bangkok, one from London, and another one.'

'Want to read them out to her?' Zade murmured sardonically, opening his mail at once, but Herbie just grinned at Catrina and handed the letters across. Zade's sarcasm usually washed right over him and he was still grinning as he left.

Catrina was not. In fact the smile left her face as soon as she saw one of the letters. She didn't actually recognise the handwriting, because Gary had never had occasion to write to her while she had known him, but she certainly recognised the postmark, and she followed Zade silently into the living-room, sitting on the settee and opening the letter as Zade sat at his desk dealing with his own mail.

It made her heart sink to get a letter from Gary because it threw her right back in time and rocked her newly acquired safety, but as she read her astonishment and downright annoyance grew. He was still trying it on, still explaining his actions and excusing them. Apparently he just *knew* she couldn't be happy in America and if she wanted to go back he would not only pay her fare, but he would come out and get her. Marriages could be broken just like engagements and he still felt the same about her.

Catrina snorted with annoyance, glaring at the letter, and her little sound of temper and disgust caught Zade's attention.

'Trouble?' He got up and sauntered over to her and she waved the letter at him.

'Trouble-maker would perhaps be a more fitting word,' she said disgustedly. 'It's a letter from Gary. Read it.'

Zade's face was no longer concerned. He looked cold and hard again.

'It's your mail,' he pointed out stiffly. 'He didn't write to both of us.'

'That won't surprise you when you see what he says. I want you to read it and then drop it on the fire.'

Zade looked at her steadily and then took the letter with obvious reluctance and Catrina paid no more attention. It had annoyed her beyond words that Gary still thought she was a mindless idiot, easily taken in, and it was clear that he was simply out to make trouble. As Zade had told her weeks ago, Gary was still simmering.

She opened one of the letters from her father and was soon absorbed in it.

'Oh! He'd like to come out to see me soon,' she said excitedly, looking up at Zade and finding his eyes fixed on her brilliantly.

'Who?' His words were almost vague and she raised her eyebrows in surprise.

'My father, of course; who else?'

'What about this?' He held out the letter from Gary and Catrina nodded to the fire that Hank had lit for the cool evening.

'You're nearest. Burn it.'

'You'll want it for when you reply,' Zade said, still with the stiffness in his voice.

'When I *what*?' Catrina looked up at him and then went back to her letter. 'If you want to reply, do so. It's your cousin, after all. And there was I blissfully thinking that any insanity was in Gary's half of the family.'

She deliberately didn't look up again and after a minute from her eye corners she saw the letter drift from Zade's hand and into the flames. Without knowing why, she felt that another bridge had been crossed, and Zade's silence as they went into town later did not trouble her at all. Once day, if he would let her, she would know him completely. For now, she could wait.

It was late when they got back. Hank had been quite taken aback that he had a free evening and the meal in town, though not up to Hank's standard, was a welcome change. Towards the end of the meal a few of Zade's friends joined them and Catrina found herself easily accepted. It was a great success and she sat sleepily in the car on the way back, not even bothered that her back was beginning to ache from all the effort of this morning's attack on the dining-room.

'What's the matter?' Zade asked later as she came from the shower in her robe and grimaced as she tried to ease aching shoulders.

'I'm stiff. And please don't say anything about it. I want to do those walls and I'm going to finish them.'

'I'm not stopping you,' he assured her quietly. 'Come here. I'll see what I can do.'

It was impossible to refuse although she would have liked to. Tonight she was more than ever tremblingly aware of Zade and her breezy attitude was all a cover for very shaken emotions. Somehow this day had been different and, although Catrina wasn't sure how the thought had come into her head, she instinctively knew. Maybe it was the worry about a pregnancy, or maybe it was Zade. Whatever it was, she walked forward reluctantly, well aware that she could so easily be hurt by any anger on his part.

He turned her away and stood behind her, his hands
on her shoulders, and she winced at the hard pressure
of strong fingers as he began to work at the muscles that
had tightened with unaccustomed exercise.

'Try to relax.' Zade's deep voice issued the order
almost huskily and it was the sound of his voice, more
than the order, that had her obeying. It would be so easy
just to melt back against him, but she did not. It would
bring about some amused comment—or even anger. It
was never possible to tell with Zade.

The tight pain eased away and her head fell in relaxation. She was almost drowsy with pleasure and when
he turned her towards him she just looked up with sleepy
eyes, submissive and dreamy, lost immediately in the
brilliant blue gaze.

'Better?' She just nodded, never taking her eyes from
him, and he began to untie her robe slowly. 'Then it's
bedtime.' He let her robe drop to the floor and when he
slid her nightie away too Catrina swayed towards him,
already melting, already feeling the great surge of fire
that Zade and only Zade brought to her blood.

He swung her up into his arms, his eyes never leaving
hers as he placed her on the bed and, discarding his own
robe, joined her there. He seemed to be content to just
look at her and Catrina looked back like some enchanted being caught in time. When his lips brushed hers
it was like listening with her whole body, waiting for
some command that would free her.

He was not kissing her. His tongue came out to lightly
touch her lips as he cupped her flushed face in strong
hands. She wanted to arch towards him, beg for more
than this, but a faint fear stilled her, the feeling that he
would reject her, smile, and tell her to sleep, as he had
done for so many nights.

A small, whimpering sound of protest escaped from her throat and Zade opened his eyes wide, looking into hers, as his hand slid down to cup her breast.

'It's all right, honey,' he murmured thickly, and his head bent until his lips found what they were searching for and he drew the swollen, aching flesh into his mouth.

Everything inside her exploded with delight, a great rush of sexual excitement that erupted deep inside and washed to every part of her. She gasped his name, her fingers reaching for his shoulders, and she felt him smile against her skin.

'Oh, you like this, don't you, Catrina? I remember just how well you like it. I remember everything you like.'

His mouth released her excited, pained breast and moved to the other, his hands restraining her as she twisted beneath him, and then his lips were hotly on her skin, his tongue tasting the rounded swell of her stomach, moving lower to probe every secret place until she was gasping and desperate, pleading with him, panic in her eyes.

'Ask me.' He raised his head and looked up at her, drowning her in blazing blue, and she reached for him agitatedly, her voice choking on the words.

'Love me! Zade! *Please!*'

'Yes. I'll love you.' His voice was deep with passion as he moved over her quickly, his lean, strong body pressing her into the softness of the bed. 'Maybe I'll love you more than you want.'

He was hard and powerful, deeply aroused, but Catrina moved convulsively against him, an almost primitive feeling inside her, desire stirring every nerve-ending.

'Zade!' She moved her head distractedly from side to side, tossing beneath him until he captured her face with hard hands, gasping to himself as her body opened willingly to his fierce invasion. She was inflamed, almost on fire, and her hands curved around his hips, urging him further, her nails digging into his skin as he began to move urgently against her.

There was a tremendous need in him that she recognised even in her dazed state and he was not being gentle. It only fed her own desire and they seemed to go wild in each other's arms.

'Catrina!' His lips fused with hers, hard and demanding, stifling her gasping cries as he took them both rushing upwards to delight. Stars seemed to shatter over her, a light as bright as the sun. The whole universe rocked and she was spinning through time, wrapped in Zade's arms, all consciousness gone.

She had no memory of drifting back to earth, but it seemed to be a long time afterwards that she opened her eyes and found Zade looking down at her, his lips tilted in a smile, his eyes burning her.

'Oh, Catrina,' he said thickly, 'you wild, wonderful creature. Devouring you would be no problem at all.'

'I'm easy to please,' she whispered with shaken humour, and his hands swept over her possessively, his eyes moving over her face.

'You know how to please me.' His eyes locked with hers for a moment and then he moved, curling her into his arms, and she sighed, drowsily satisfied, totally relaxed.

'I suppose it's up early in the morning as usual?' she murmured, her face against his shoulder.

'Maybe not. I might just lie here until Hank turns me out. I might just keep all the boys waiting for once.'

'Will you be out all day?' she asked wistfully, and he drew back to look down at her.

'Will you mind?' His gaze was probing, questioning, but she dared not say what was in her heart.

'I'll manage.' She smiled up at him and his fingers trailed over her face, giving her courage to ask her own question.

'Zade. Why?' She didn't need to say more. His face told her that he understood without further explanation. She was asking herself why he had made love to her tonight when he had left her alone for so long.

'Because today was different,' he said softly. 'Today you almost told me what I want to know.'

'Almost?' When he simply nodded she stared up at him, wide-eyed.

'Then tell me what you want to know.'

'No, Catrina. I can wait. Go to sleep.'

It was frustrating. There was something at the back of his eyes that she wanted to find out about, something she needed to know, and here he was, telling her to go to sleep.

'I'm not tired,' she said crossly. She was not. She was still singing inside, still wildly alive, and sleep had never seemed so far away.

'So what are you going to do—read a book?' There was a taunting look in his eyes, a drowsy sexual appraisal, and Catrina flushed wildly as he slowly ran his hand down her body, his fingers flexing against her flesh.

She shivered in delight, immediately melting against him, and he turned her into his arms, his eyes holding hers.

'What do you want, Star-eyes?' he asked seriously, and she closed her eyes, her hands coming to touch his face, her fingertips tracing his skin, every part of her tingling.

'Love me, Zade,' she begged softly. 'Love me again.' And she was instantly crushed against him, his lips hard on hers, his breathing harshly demanding, as he moved over her and gathered her close.

CHAPTER TEN

THE days had been sunny now for some time, the ranch taking on an altogether different look. As the snow cleared, Catrina discovered a garden round the house, a garden that Zade's mother had carefully nurtured. It was a small discovery, but it added to her growing happiness. She was really Zade's wife now and rarely saw the cold, hard look in his eyes that she had thought was natural to him. He might not love her, but he wanted her; she seemed to be necessary to his existence.

She felt very close to Zade's mother and Bart Mackensie treated her like a long-lost child. She was getting to know the men who worked around the ranch and Stella had not been near since her brush with Jean.

The dining-room was finished and even Bart approved. Catrina felt that she was beginning to be part of the place and she loved it all the more because it was Zade's place. The happiness she had never expected to find was growing daily.

There was an air of elation about the ranch one morning as she got up. Zade had left very early and as she was having breakfast he came into the kitchen and leaned over her chair, looking down into her flushed face with glittering-eyed satisfaction.

'Want to come out and see a bit of excitement?' he enquired softly. 'We've brought the horses in.'

It was enough to have Catrina jumping up and abandoning her breakfast, and even Hank didn't scowl. He trailed along behind, a glint in his eyes that almost amounted to glee. Catrina knew why. Next week the spring round-up would begin. Everything would come to life and the horses were a very necessary part of the event. There might be a helicopter and numerous pick-ups, but on the wide acres of the Mackensie Ranch horses were still essential.

The big corrals behind the sheds had been repaired over the past few days and as Catrina walked with Zade towards them she could see that they were filled with horses—bays, sorrels, buckskins and greys—all milling around with restless energy. They were not unbroken, as Zade had told her earlier, but they were overflowing with mischief after weeks of being underworked.

About ten men were ranged around the corrals, leaning against the rails, eyeing the horses expertly. Extra men would be taken on for the round-up and Zade's own crew were getting their pick in first because each man would need at least four horses.

'What am *I* supposed to do?' Herbie Moore turned rather anxiously from his perch on the top rail of the corral. 'Riding them is one thing; catching them is another.'

'I'll get yours this time, or Jerry will,' Zade promised, lifting Catrina lightly to the rail beside Herbie. 'After this, though, you're on your own. You can learn a lot by watching the old hands pick out their string.'

Zade watched too, standing close to Catrina, and she soon forgot everything. It was so exciting. The men took turns to go among the horses, their ropes in a wide loop as they pursued the horse of their choice, and it was not easy. The horses moved away fast, packing themselves against the rails, turning their backs as if they were well aware of the difficulty this presented. Their ears were flattened back, their nostrils wide. They had no in-tention of being caught.

It took skill and patience, but as Catrina watched each horse finally cornered and roped, saw the way they gave in as the flying loop settled over their neck and they felt the weight of the man behind it as he dug his heels into the ground, she began to think that with a bit of practice she could do it herself.

She muttered this lofty thought to Herbie and to her great chagrin he roared it out to Zade above the noise of singing ropes and stamping hoofs.

'We'll get the hacking dealt with first,' Zade suggested with a grin. She found herself laughing down into his vivid eyes and then as she turned quickly back to the exciting scene a great wave of dizziness swept over her. It was the first time since that day in the dining-room and she was quite unprepared for it. She could feel herself falling and there was nothing she could do about it at all.

The speed with which Zade moved was astonishing. She was swept off the rail and into his arms before Herbie had even noticed her distress.

'Again?' Zade enquired grimly, staring into her white face. 'I think you've had enough for today, Catrina.'

'I—I'm all right, really,' she pleaded, a little colour coming back into her face. 'It was the movement, the dust, all those horses milling around, and I was sitting right over them. It was enough to make anybody dizzy'

'I don't see Herbie falling off the fence,' Zade pointed out quietly. 'Last time it was being hungry, as I understand it. This time it's movement. Are you working on our next excuse?'

He was watching her so intently that she was sure he knew and her pale cheeks flushed with confusion.

'I think you should put me down,' she whispered anxiously. 'Everybody will be looking.'

'Well, Herbie's interested,' Zade agreed, glancing up. 'The others are too busy.' He let her stand, all the same. 'Think you can walk to the house?'

'I'm staying!' Catrina assured him determinedly, gripping the rail nearest to her with tight fingers. 'I want to watch you catch Herbie's horses.'

For a moment their eyes locked in silent battle, but to her joy he shrugged and gave in.

'You stand, however,' he ordered. 'That way if you hit the ground it's not so far to fall and nothing's going to stamp on you.'

Catrina was happy to agree and she had the pleasure then of watching Zade work the horses. Jerry Brennan, the foreman and husband of Liz, came up to her as she watched.

'We left him the meanest,' he told her with a grin.

'It's not making much difference,' Herbie said proudly. 'The boss can do anything.'

'Sure can,' Jerry agreed wryly. 'Just remember though that he's catching yours. A mean horse is a mean ride.'

It silenced Herbie and Catrina watched Zade with starry eyes. Everything he did was perfect to her. She didn't need anyone to point out his perfection. She was still looking like that when he came back and climbed over the rails to stand beside her, his eyes slanting across her face with the same brilliance.

'Don't do it,' he warned softly. 'It's sure to bring retaliation.'

When she blushed and turned away he lifted her to the bottom rail so that she could lean her arms along the top and watch more easily and she was shiveringly aware that he stood behind her, his hands on either side of her. It was probably so that she wouldn't get dizzy again, but it was very close.

They were standing like that when Stella arrived. She had evidently parked by the house and walked round and now she came forward confidently, pushing her way between Zade and Herbie and almost knocking the irritated young man off the rails.

'You're one up on us,' she confessed, smiling at Zade. 'We do this tomorrow.' She looked at Catrina and smiled more widely. 'Scared to sit up on the top rail?'

'She's been there,' Zade murmured before Catrina could think of an answer. 'I'd rather have her here.' He bent his head and brushed his lips against Catrina's black curls. 'It's more cosy.'

Catrina was ridiculously grateful to him for not mentioning her dizzy feeling. She wanted Stella to know nothing about her at all. Even now there was a proprietorial air about Stella Cunningham when she spoke to Zade. It might have been years of knowing him, but she gave the impression of knowing him too well. And her gratitude was mixed with worry, too. Zade was not demonstrative when there were others present. Was he making some private point to Stella?

If he was, she didn't seem to take it to heart.

'Jean used to arrange a party before spring round-up,' she informed Catrina, her eyes narrowed as she watched Zade's arms tighten almost imperceptibly. It was that act that gave Catrina courage.

'What a marvellous idea! It would start events off with a swing. I'll arrange it at once.'

'I'll be there,' Stella said smugly, a veiled threat in her eyes that Catrina saw all too well.

Later, Zade brought the subject up.

'If you're set on having a party you'll have to move fast,' he pointed out. 'Pretty soon every man on the ranches will be scattered over a thousand acres.'

'I'll do it,' Catrina said firmly. 'I didn't know there was a tradition. Why didn't you tell me?' She always felt ruffled and unsure when she had been anywhere near Stella Cunningham and as usual she stiffened up with Zade, wanting reassurance and getting none at all.

'I thought you might not be up to it,' he confessed quietly, his voice hardening at her tone.

'You mean up to it physically or up to it emotionally?' Catrina asked crossly, still smarting from Stella's possessive way with Zade.

He just looked at her and then turned away, heading for the door and his work.

'Don't pick a fight with me, Catrina,' he warned softly 'I might not take kindly to it. If Stella's bothering you deal with her.'

Catrina stared after him bleakly. How could she deal with Stella when she didn't know how things had been before she came here? How did she know that Zade had not simply married her because he wanted her more than he wanted Stella? She supposed that thought should have comforted her, but it didn't. She wanted Zade to love her as she loved him and he showed no sign of doing that.

When she mentioned the party Jean Mackensie got very excited and started to help with the organisation at once.

'We've always had it in the big barn,' she said. 'You get more people in that way. There are lanterns and bunting all stored away. I'll get on the phone for you this afternoon. Nobody expects an invitation card.'

'Suppose they don't come as I've left it so late?' Catrina asked glumly, wondering if it would make Zade look a fool.

'They'll come, love,' Jean gurgled. 'They all expect it. Bart's mother started it and I kept it going. Tradition Nobody else will have thought to prepare one.'

'What about all the cooking?' Catrina asked, her mind on Hank's peculiarities.

'Everybody brings something because when you get right down to it it's a barn dance. There's quite a bit of musical talent spread out across the ranches, too. We have our own band. The boys put up the bunting and arrange bales of straw to sit on. All you do is walk about and point.'

'I couldn't do that!' Catrina gasped.

'Of course you can; you're Zade's wife.'

It seemed to be something that would give her energy and stamina, let alone glory, and Catrina hoped she could live up to it. This was a far cry from her quiet life in the dale. Here, things happened on a large scale to match the landscape. At the moment she felt extremely insignificant because, after her brush with him, Zade was somewhat terse with her. His arms didn't reach out for her at all.

When the day arrived she had great difficulty in keeping calm. To her surprise Hank had shown enthusiasm and he was in the barn when she got there.

'Leave it to me, Miz Mackensie,' he said with more happiness than she had ever seen him show. 'I know what happens. Folks will bring their cakes and things and I'll set them up here.'

He had two long trestle-tables at one end of the barn and already she could see the beginnings of a party taking shape. The bunting was up and two of the boys were moving the bales to the sides of the barn.

'OK, Mrs Mackensie?' Herbie grinned at her from the top of a huge bale and she waved to him before turning round to Hank.

'I hope it's going to be as good as usual,' she murmured, and he surprised her again by actually chuckling.

'Better,' he assured her drily. 'There's nobody that won't be outdoing themselves to show Zade's new wife what they're made of. Saw it happen when Bart brought his new wife. This time they'll do more. I got steaks sizzling already, nothing to worry about.'

Coming from Hank, it was a great boost to her confidence, and she went off to get changed in an easier frame of mind. It would have been better if she could have told Zade about her worries, but he seemed very distant since their small spat and she felt that every bit of responsibility was on her shoulders.

When she came down the stairs later Zade was in the hall and he looked up, watching her as she came down reluctantly. He was in grey trousers, a white shirt brilliant against his tanned skin, and he stared at her for a second before saying, 'Going to be warm enough?' She was in a pale turquoise dress, softly printed with flowers, the wide, swinging skirt easy for dancing.

'I hope so. Your mother said it gets hot in the barn.'

'Let's go.' He made no further comment and she walked beside him round to the barn, her heart fluttering ridiculously. There was no need at all for this attack of nerves. She knew most people now. Childishly, though, she wanted Zade's praise. She wanted him to tell her that she looked pretty. She wanted his arm round her, protecting her, but he made no move to grant her secret wishes.

They had already put lights on and there were even fairy lights across the roof. The coloured bunting was fluttering in the rising air currents and Catrina breathed an audible sigh of relief. It looked good, a very warm party scene. She could already smell Hank's cooking and he was right there, his white apron firmly fastened. She crossed her fingers. Now all she needed was guests and a bit of luck.

The guests arrived, more than she had imagined. They were soon pouring in through the barn doors, laughing and noisy, greeting her as she stood with Zade, carrying baskets to Hank and having a good time before the evening had even started. Cars seemed to be arriving every second and Catrina had to agree with Jean, who came across as soon as she arrived and hugged her.

'Well, if anything goes wrong, nobody's going to notice in this crowd.' It was a great consolation and just about settled Catrina's nerves. When the music started and Zade came to look for her she relaxed and started to enjoy herself.

She wasn't even allowed to sit out when the square dancing started. Zade dragged her along and she had to learn fast. With the constant changing of partners she met plenty of other people and soon every worry was forgotten. Forgotten until she saw Stella arrive and urge Zade from the circle and away from the crowd.

They were probably only going to get a drink. After all, Zade could hardly ignore her without creating a scene. Catrina told herself this firmly, but it did nothing to cheer her up, and it did nothing to prevent her eyes roaming back to them frequently.

She hated the way Zade stood, tall and handsome, laughing down into Stella's upturned face. She hated her own wild jealousy and the way it tore at her like an actual pain. Whatever they were saying to each other seemed to be deeply intimate and Catrina was almost tearfully grateful when Herbie claimed her for a very fast dance that entailed being spun round vigorously.

When they stopped Stella was right there beside them and Herbie wandered off, leaving Catrina to face the amused green eyes.

'Well, it's a good party,' she congratulated wryly. 'You're really trying hard.'

'Being here is very different from home,' Catrina managed evenly. She was hot, tired after all the dancing and the worry, and she longed to call to Jean to rescue her. 'I seem to be fitting in, though.'

'As a novelty, you probably are,' Stella acknowledged with quiet spite. 'Novelties wear off, though. I've seen novelties wear off before with Zade. He always comes back to me.'

'Zade is now married,' Catrina managed in a choked voice. 'That kind of novelty doesn't wear off.'

'We'll see,' Stella promised complacently, and everything in Catrina boiled over—her hurt, her jealousy, and her pain at not having Zade's love.

'I don't think we will, Miss Cunningham,' she said heatedly. 'There's a new novelty on the way—Zade's child. When it arrives, I don't think I want to see you anywhere around it. Get used to staying away from the ranch. As far as I can see you're a pain to everyone and *I* certainly don't welcome you!'

For a second she thought Stella was going to strike her—in fact she was quite prepared for it—because the green eyes blazed furiously at her, and then the other woman turned and walked off, stiff with rage, heading straight for Zade.

'Anything wrong, ma'am?' Jerry Brennan came across to her, his keen eyes alert, and she managed to smile at him, although her face felt cold and rigid.

'No, nothing, thank you, Jerry. I...I...'

Without even the warning of dizziness, she fainted, pitching forward into Jerry's arms, her last sight of things Zade's face as he pushed his way through the dancers towards her.

When she came round she was outside the barn in the cooler air. Zade was holding her and Jean and Bart were standing by anxiously. Catrina looked dazedly up at Zade and he looked back grimly.

'The party's over for you,' he assured her with no sign whatever that he would relent.

'I...I can't just leave...'

'You're going to have one hell of a time getting back in past me,' he rasped. He seemed angry and Jean came forward quickly.

'Don't worry, love,' she said. 'Bart and I will keep things going to the end. It's nearly time to finish anyway and most people know you fainted. As soon as I tell them you're all right they'll get back on with the party and leave a few at a time later. They always do.'

'They've got two chances,' Zade muttered, starting off to the house with Catrina. 'I'll leave you to it, Mom. Goodnight, Bart; I'll be in touch tomorrow.'

'You'll have to go back to the party,' Catrina protested, and he merely glanced down at her grimly.

'What party?' He said nothing more and he refused to let her walk. Catrina felt that she had in some minor way produced a catastrophe.

Upstairs, he placed her on the bed, pulling off her shoes and plumping the pillows up behind her. She hoped he might just walk out, because he did not look in any way encouraging. He did not walk out. He stood looking down at her and then said quietly,

'Don't imagine you're getting away without seeing the doctor this time. First thing in the morning I take you to town.'

'I don't need a doctor,' Catrina informed him, looking away from his intent and annoyed eyes.

'I believe you do. If you imagine I'm going to wait until you faint again, forget it. Next time it might be at the top of the stairs.'

'I'll take care.'

'No doubt! The doctor will insist on it—after he's had a look at you.'

'I...I don't need a doctor, Zade,' she said tremulously, anxious about his reaction to her confession. 'I'm...I'm pregnant.'

'Oh, I figured that out for myself, being a country boy,' he assured her icily. 'I felt I could wait for you to tell me in your own good time. What I didn't expect was that you would tell Stella first.'

Catrina looked at him tragically. What was he saying? Did he mean that he was angry about Stella knowing? She would have to know some time; everybody would.

'I would never have told her if she hadn't said the things to me that she did. You told me to deal with her. It was the only way I had.' Tears came to her eyes, but she looked up at him angrily. 'Was I expected to just stand there when she told me I was a novelty that would wear off, just like your other novelties? She said you always go back to her so...so I——'

'Flattened her with facts?'

He looked at her with piercing blue eyes and she turned away, sliding down and turning her head into the pillow.

'It was all I had.'

'Was it? I thought you had me. That seems to be a fact that escaped you.' He was silent for a minute and Catrina dared not look at him. Then she felt him sit beside her, his hands coming to her shoulders as he turned her to face him.

'Yes,' he said quietly. 'You're a novelty all right. You never look at the things that are right under your nose. You seem quite content to believe any lunatic who can come up with a good story.' He lifted her up, cupping her face in his hands, forcing her to meet his eyes. 'I couldn't go *back* to Stella because I've never been to her in the first place. A woman who stamps around telling me what to do with my own life on my own spread does not and never has appealed to me. I married the particular novelty I wanted, even though she seems extremely reluctant to have my baby.'

'I'm not!' Catrina stared at him in horror. 'How could you think that?'

'What did you expect me to think when you kept it from me? I assumed that if you were happy about it you would have wanted to share it with me. I'm not an idiot, Catrina, and I can count. I've given you every chance to tell me, but you didn't. I could only think that you hated the idea.'

'Why do you always assume the worst?' Catrina stormed, snatching her face away and glaring at him, her cheeks flushed with temper. 'I just felt insecure, that's all.' Her voice rose and she almost shouted at him. 'Any woman wants to have the baby of the man she loves.'

She was too cross to realise exactly what she had said, but Zade's mouth tilted in a smile, and his eyes moved over her flushed and angry face.

'Temper brings out the Italian in you,' he said quietly. 'At this moment those soft brown eyes are black and flashing.' He caught her towards him, stilling her struggles with strong, patient hands. 'Temper leaves your tongue unguarded too. I was beginning to wonder if I'd have to wait for years to hear you say you loved me.'

'I...I never said it,' Catrina protested.

'Yes, you did, Mrs Mackensie, and you'll say it again plenty of times. Now you've told me everything I wanted to hear.' His hand smoothed over her black curls and he drew her closer, cradling her against him. 'There's no need to look so frantic,' he whispered. 'I'm quite crazy about my wife.'

'You are?' She looked up at him with bewildered longing and he smiled down at her.

'I am. Why do you think I was so set on marrying you? I was even crazy enough to force you into marrying me.' His lips brushed hers gently and he lifted his head to look down at her. 'I love you, Star-eyes.'

'Oh, Zade!' Catrina linked her arms around his neck, submitting gladly to the kisses he scattered across her face and neck, her lips opening sweetly when he claimed them.

'Why didn't you tell me?' she asked rather mournfully when her lips were burning and he held her in the curve of his arm.

'You told me repeatedly that you loved Gary. Even on that last day you were forgiving him, moving towards him. I held you in my arms all night and next day he came and began to get round you with no effort at all.'

'He didn't,' Catrina assured him seriously. 'I was just standing there stunned, listening to the same old story. If you saw anything at all on my face it was astonishment at my own stupidity. Besides,' she added, blushing and looking away, 'I already knew what the magic was. I already knew I loved you. That was why I burned whenever you were near. That was why it was only you I could respond to.'

'So it wasn't just chemistry that animals have?' he enquired drily, reminding her of her sharp words to him in the past. 'That hit me really hard. I was standing there, worshipping you, and you gave me a lecture on love. It was love you felt for Gary, chemistry for me. Did you expect me to confess then how I felt about you?'

'Oh, Zade! Can't we forget it?' she begged, and he smiled wryly.

'In about ten years, unless you're prepared to do a lot of penance in the meantime.'

'Any penance you like,' she promised softly, closing her eyes against the startling blue of his.

'You can begin tonight—if you're up to it,' he murmured against her skin. 'Pretty soon, though, I think we'll be having anxious visitors. My mother and Bart dote on their new daughter-in-law. They may be keeping the party going, but I know where their minds are lingering. Better sit up and look healthy because they'll be up here soon enough. I wouldn't be surprised to see Hank sticking his head round the door.'

'What about Stella?' Catrina asked worriedly. 'I told her not to come here again.'

'So?' He slanted her a look of amusement. 'You deal with her. It saves me the trouble.'

'She's an... an old friend...'

'Forget her.' He stood and looked down at her with a smile. 'I love you, Catrina. You're the boss here—when I'm out.' He went downstairs, leaving her glowing with happiness. Zade loved her. The magic was real.

Later, when all the cars had gone and the shadows of night had settled across the prairie, Catrina lay, sweetly happy, in Zade's arms. There were no shadows between them now and Zade had shown her how much he loved her. There were questions, though, and Catrina asked them as she snuggled up to Zade, her head on his shoulder.

'Why did you go back to Kellerdale after six years away?'

'You,' he said quietly. 'I told you that coming back for the last time was a duty. It was a duty to you, although I never dreamed it would mean everything to me.'

'You didn't even know me!' Catrina looked up and he smiled down into her eyes.

'No. I'd only seen you once, and that very briefly. I knew Gary, though, and if I hadn't come back I guess it would have haunted me for the rest of my life.'

When she just looked puzzled he drew her close, his head against her shining curls.

'Six years ago,' he explained, 'I decided I'd had more than enough of Gary. Over the years he simply got worse and it was time I cut my ties with Kellerdale and the past anyway. It was to be my last visit. My mind was quite made up on that. I got the usual thing from Gary—the great deeds he'd done, the women in his life... and there were plenty. My aunt only got more sour with the years and I asked myself what on earth I was doing there after all—looking for something I'd gladly given up in my teens.

'On my last day, I saw you. Perhaps I wouldn't have noticed you in town, but Gary noticed. All week I'd been hearing about the new interest, the latest arrival in the dale, and he suddenly said, "There she is. I'll let you know when I've got round her."

'He was laughing, pointing across the road, and I expected some sight of his usual type of woman—brassy, worldly and willing. When I saw you I felt almost sick. I wanted to turn round and knock him flat. You were coming out of a shop with your father, clinging to his arm, smiling, and I had to admit that I'd never seen a girl like you before. You were eighteen, sweet, innocent, beautiful and hopelessly vulnerable. All I could do was growl at Gary and tell him you were not his type, too young anyway. He thought it was highly amusing. He just said, "I'll get round her."

'I almost felt like coming across to warn you, but I had a close look at your father. He was a big man, self-assured and quiet, obviously nobody's fool. I told myself you were safe because, apart from anything else, you were light-years above Gary.'

He sounded so angry at the memory that Catrina put her hand against his face, reaching up to kiss him.

'I was safe,' she told him softly. 'There was my mother too. The three of us were very happy. We saw the cottage when we were on a brief holiday and my mother was so taken with it that we moved.' She smiled up at him. 'If we hadn't, I would never have met you.'

'Stop frightening me,' Zade growled, tightening his arms around her.

'But how did you know what was happening?'

'Oh, Gary wrote to me frequently in those days. At first there was no mention of you and I breathed a sigh of relief. I assumed he'd been given the cold shoulder. I imagined you were safe. I even let you drift from my mind.'

'Didn't you go on dreaming about me?' Catrina asked mournfully, and he grinned down at her, dropping a kiss on the tip of her nose.

'I'm not the dreamy type. In any case, I don't chase teenagers. You were safe and I forgot almost completely.' His face hardened. 'Then I had a letter. He was engaged, getting married in May, and there was some sort of triumph in the letter too that made my blood run cold. "You remember that girl I pointed out when you were over here? I told you I'd get round her. She'll be my wife in about four months' time." I remembered you then. All I felt was a sort of gloomy disappointment that you'd turned out like the rest, not able to work out just what Gary was. If you were engaged to him then you were no sort of innocent either. I had been quite wrong about you.'

'But you came all the same?' Catrina asked softly.

'I came.' He turned her towards him, stroking back her hair and smiling into her eyes. 'I couldn't get it out of my mind. I had to find out.'

'I thought you were summing me up as suitable for Gary.'

'I was summing you up,' he admitted wryly. 'What I hadn't bargained for was the effect you would have on me. You were grown-up. You stunned me, took my breath away, and that first night when you pointed out grimly that you were not yet married I had the terrible feeling that he was just marrying you to satisfy his ego. You were the one who refused him. It seemed to be just part of some strategy to get you.'

'You worried me,' Catrina confessed. 'You seemed to separate me from Gary without doing anything at all. I couldn't understand it.'

'I couldn't understand why you went on saying you loved him when you were ready to fall into my arms,' Wade told her seriously. 'I knew there was no way I was leaving without you. I was quite prepared to trick you into marrying me.'

'I wouldn't exactly call it a trick,' Catrina pointed out demurely, blushing at the look in his eyes.

'No,' he agreed softly. 'It was more of a pleasure, the greatest in my life. By that time I loved you so much I would have given up the ranch and just stayed there. I had to get you away, though, away from the danger of Gary and the hurt that everyone else seemed to be determined to fling in your direction.' He leaned over her, his lips drifting across her face, catching her mouth, and filling her with the same joyous excitement. 'I wanted you badly, Catrina, and I wanted to take care of you, to cherish you always as you deserve to be cherished.'

'After that night, you never touched me. You even put me into that room next door.'

'I told myself I would never touch you again until I felt you loved me. Sleeping with you and not making love to you was something I couldn't take.'

'But you brought me in here the next night.'

'I couldn't have Stella or anyone else hurting you. It meant a lot of self-discipline, though. When Gary wrote and you reacted as you did, I felt we were almost there.' He grinned down at her. 'Anyway, that was my excuse.'

'Do you want this baby?' Catrina asked breathlessly, melting against him and winding her arms around his neck.

'Do you?' he whispered.

'Oh, yes, Zade! It's yours. I love you.'

'Then I'll share you,' he promised tenderly. 'Whatever you want, I want, darling.'

He pulled her closer still and she was soon lost in the magic that flowed between them. She knew that Zade felt it too and he smiled down at the look on her face.

'Wild and gentle. What a combination,' he said huskily. 'You've got the boys eating out of your hand you've turned Hank into a soft-hearted idiot, and you've got me so that I couldn't care less if this round-up takes place or not.'

'But you can do anything,' Catrina assured him mischievously. 'You're the boss.'

'Only until I look at you, darling,' he said thickly. 'Then I'm not sure who I am. All I want to do is stay close to you.'

'Let's hope for a long, hard winter,' Catrina murmured comfortingly, and their laughter mingled as his lips claimed hers.

Catrina knelt in the garden, weeding vigorously, the sunlight catching her shining black curls. After a moment she sat back on her heels and breathed in the sweet, fresh air. Happiness was intoxicating and it ran through her blood like wine. She looked across at the child who played contentedly on a thick rug spread on the lawn, a child who was a mirror image of herself—Zade's daughter.

It was time for the spring round-up again and the past year had sped by on golden wings.

'Nearly lunchtime,' she confided. 'When I've just done this, we'll eat.'

'*Past* lunchtime,' a voice corrected, and Catrina raised a flushed, happy face as Zade stood over her, looking mockingly severe.

'It's not going to be long,' she laughed. 'Hank's getting it right now.'

'I suppose he's been out here all morning,' Zade surmised. 'When I asked about lunch he said it would be ready—sooner or later.' He dropped to the rug and stared thoughtfully at the baby who watched him with dark eyes. 'Elizabeth Mackensie, you cause as much trouble as your mother.'

'She's good as gold,' Catrina protested, standing and brushing off her jeans.

'It's not her, it's Hank,' Zade corrected, pulling her down to him on the rug and looking up into her laughing eyes. 'He's taken on too much—nursemaid to my two women, ruler of the kitchen and general busybody. He's getting unbearable.'

'Well, he says you work too hard,' Catrina informed him, resting on her elbows and looking down into the brilliant eyes. 'With the round-up here you'll be busy from morning to night.'

'You'll all have to cope,' Zade murmured, his gaze on her smiling mouth. 'I seem to remember a long, hard winter,' he added sensuously. 'You never complained then.'

'I'm not complaining now,' Catrina said, waiting for the kiss that was certain to come. 'It's just that I want to see you all the time. We miss you.'

'You and Hank?' Zade's arm shot out and captured his daughter as she began to stealthily crawl away. He pulled her close to them and looked with amusement at the likeness. 'Two of you,' he said softly. 'I never expected so much happiness.' He pulled Catrina down closer, brushing her lips with his.

'A boy would probably look like you,' Catrina whispered, and felt his lips smile against her own.

'Is that what we're having?' he murmured into her mouth, and she shot up, looking down at him crossly.

'How do you know? I hardly know myself yet!'

'I told you,' Zade grinned. 'It comes of being a country boy.' His hand curved round her nape and he began to kiss her hungrily, his other arm holding their delighted daughter, who tried to wriggle free.

'Going to be all day?' Hank demanded from the edge of the lawn. 'Think I've nothing better to do than hang around waiting?'

They followed him into the house laughing, their arms round each other, Elizabeth in the curve of Zade's arm, and in the doorway Catrina stopped and looked back, across the garden to the hills, the distant mountains. She loved all this. She belonged here. Zade looked down at her, his eyes smiling as he kissed the tip of her nose.

'I love you, Catrina,' he said gently. 'I love everything about you, but you already know that, don't you?'

She reached up to kiss him. She knew. They went inside together and outside the rolling landscape glowed in the sun. The quiet of the prairie was peaceful, timeless, but inside there was magic, the only kind of magic, a joyous, lasting love.

BRIDE'S
BAY RESORT

UNLOCK THE DOOR TO GREAT ROMANCE
AT BRIDE'S BAY RESORT

Join Harlequin's new across-the-lines series, set in an exclusive hotel on an island off the coast of South Carolina.

Seven of your favorite authors will bring you exciting stories about fascinating heroes and heroines discovering love at Bride's Bay Resort.

Look for these fabulous stories coming to a store near you beginning in January 1996.

Harlequin American Romance #613 in January
Matchmaking Baby by Cathy Gillen Thacker

Harlequin Presents #1794 in February
Indiscretions by Robyn Donald

Harlequin Intrigue #362 in March
Love and Lies by Dawn Stewardson

Harlequin Romance #3404 in April
Make Believe Engagement by Day Leclaire

Harlequin Temptation #588 in May
Stranger in the Night by Roseanne Williams

Harlequin Superromance #695 in June
Married to a Stranger by Connie Bennett

Harlequin Historicals #324 in July
Dulcie's Gift by Ruth Langan

Visit Bride's Bay Resort each month wherever
Harlequin books are sold.

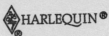

HARLEQUIN ®

BBAYG

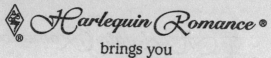

Harlequin Romance ®

brings you

HOLDING
HER★
OUT FOR A

Some men are worth waiting for!

They're handsome, they're charming but, best of all,
they're single! Twelve lucky women are about to
discover that finding Mr. Right is not a problem—it's
holding on to him.

In May the series continues with:

#3408 MOVING IN WITH ADAM
by Jeanne Allan

Hold out for Harlequin Romance's heroes in
coming months...

♦ June: **THE DADDY TRAP**—Leigh Michaels
♦ July: **THE BACHELOR'S WEDDING**—Betty Neels
♦ August: **KIT AND THE COWBOY**—Rebecca Winters

HOFH-5

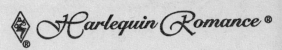

New from Harlequin Romance
a very special six-book series by

MIDNIGHT SONS
DEBBIE MACOMBER

The town of Hard Luck, Alaska, needs women!

The O'Halloran brothers, who run a bush-plane service called Midnight Sons, are heading a campaign to attract women to Hard Luck. *(Location: north of the Arctic Circle. Population: 150—mostly men!)*

"Debbie Macomber's *Midnight Sons* series is a delightful romantic saga. And each book is a powerful, engaging story in its own right. Unforgettable!"

—Linda Lael Miller

TITLE IN THE MIDNIGHT SONS SERIES:

DMS-1

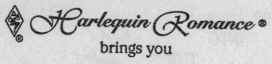

Harlequin Romance ®

brings you

How the West Was Wooed!

We've rounded up twelve of our most popular
authors, and the result is a whole year of
romance, Western style. Every month we'll be
bringing you a spirited, independent woman
whose heart is about to be lassoed by a rugged,
handsome, one-hundred-percent cowboy!

Watch for...

♦ May: THE BADLANDS BRIDE—Rebecca Winters

♦ June: RUNAWAY WEDDING—Ruth Jean Dale

♦ July: A RANCH, A RING AND EVERYTHING—Val Daniels

♦ August: TEMPORARY TEXAN—Heather Allison

Available wherever Harlequin books are sold.

HITCH-4

STEP

INTO

THE

WINNER'S CIRCLE

A collection of award-winning books
by award-winning authors!
From Harlequin and Silhouette.

Available this May

A Human Touch
by Glenda Sanders

VOTED BEST SHORT CONTEMPORARY ROMANCE—*RITA AWARD WINNER*

When dire circumstances force together a single mother with
an adorable one-month-old baby and an arrogant lawyer,
emotions start to get out of control as *A Human Touch* proves
to have a powerful effect on their lives.

"Glenda Sanders weaves a masterful spell..."
—*Inside Romance*

Available this May wherever Harlequin books are sold.

WC-5